D0049401

illyria

BOOKS BY ELIZABETH HAND

Winterlong

Aestival Tide

Icarus Descending

Waking the Moon

Glimmering

Last Summer at Mars Hill (short stories)

Black Light

Bibliomancy (novellas)

Mortal Love

Chip Crockett's Christmas Carol

Saffron and Brimstone (short stories)

Generation Loss

Illyria

illyria

a novel by

ELIZABETH HAND

VIKING

An Imprint of Penguin Group (USA) Inc.

VIKING

Published by Penguin Group
Penguin Group (USA) Inc., 345 Hudson Street, New York, New York 10014, U.S.A.
Penguin Group (Canada), 90 Eglinton Avenue East, Suite 700, Toronto, Ontario, Canada M4P 2Y3
(a division of Pearson Penguin Canada Inc.)
Penguin Books Ltd, 80 Strand, London WC2R 0RL, England
Penguin Ireland, 25 St Stephen's Green, Dublin 2, Ireland (a division of Penguin Books Ltd.)
Penguin Group (Australia), 250 Camberwell Road, Camberwell, Victoria 3124, Australia
(a division of Pearson Australia Group Pty Ltd.)
Penguin Books India Pvt Ltd., 11 Community Centre, Panchsheel Park, New Delhi – 110 017, India
Penguin Group (NZ), 67 Apollo Drive, Rosedale, North Shore 0632, New Zealand
(a division of Pearson New Zealand Ltd.)
Penguin Books (South Africa) (Pty) Ltd, 24 Sturdee Avenue, Rosebank, Johannesburg 2196, South Africa

Penguin Books Ltd., Registered Offices: 80 Strand, London WC2R 0RL, England

First published in the United Kingdom in 2007 by PS Publishing Ltd.

First published in the United States in 2010 by Viking, a member of Penguin Group (USA) Inc.

1 3 5 7 9 10 8 6 4 2

Copyright © Elizabeth Hand, 2007, 2010
All rights reserved

LIBRARY OF CONGRESS CATALOGING-IN-PUBLICATION DATA IS AVAILABLE
ISBN: 978-0-670-01212-1

Printed in U.S.A.
Set in Minion
Book design by Sam Kim

For Russell Dunn,
who made it real, then and now

illyria

R OGAN AND I WERE COUSINS; OUR FATHERS were identical twins. Rogan was the youngest of six boys, I the youngest of six girls. Growing up, there were always jokes about this symmetry, even though everyone in the Tierney clan bred prolifically—there were twenty-six first cousins, divided among five families.

Still, only Rogan and I were ever called kissing cousins, despite the fact that our older brothers and sisters were also paired off, agewise, as neatly as if our parents had timed their conjugal relations so that their children would all be born within a few days of each other, and Rogan and I actually on the same day. I arrived in the early morning, Rogan moments before midnight. Later, when we were adolescents, the facts of our birth (we always thought of it as *our* birth) conveniently fulfilled our need to find meaning in everything about ourselves.

So Rogan was darkness, I was light, and over the years the metaphor was extended to include just about every doomy literary reference you can imagine—Caliban and Ariel, Peter Pan and Wendy, Heathcliff and Cathy, Abelard and Heloise, Tristan and Iseult, Evnissyen and Nissyen . . .

You get the idea.

Ours had been a noted theatrical clan, a line of performers stretching back to Shakespeare's day. Our great-grandmother was the once-famous actress Madeline Armin Tierney. I was her namesake. Yeats was rumored to have written his poem "The Last Stone of Carrowkeel" for Madeline, and our aunt Kate claimed that the character of Caitilin Ni Murrachu in James Stephens's *The Crock of Gold* was inspired by her, as well.

But the family forsook the stage. Madeline gave up acting when she married. Her children and grandchildren regarded the theater with a mixture of bemusement and condescension, fear and guilt, the same emotions stirred by the even rarer mention of sex.

Only Aunt Kate dwelled on this abandonment with grim persistence.

"Like cutting down a tree in its prime," she'd tell Rogan and me, the only two who ever listened. "Nothing good ever comes of that. Never ever ever."

There were remnants of family history scattered throughout our homes at Arden Terrace. Framed billets advertising performances by Edwin Booth or Otis Skinner or Charlotte Cushman, with various Tierneys in supporting roles. Peter Pangloss in *The Heir at Law*, Madame Trentoni in *Captain Jinks*; the Fool, Hermione, Dogberry. A lurid painting of a nameless ancestor as one of the witches in *Macbeth*. Mother-of-pearl opera glasses, silver spoons engraved with obscure jokes: "To His Highness from a Rogue."

We retained theatrical superstitions, as well, unmoored from their element and thus meaningless. Peacock feathers were banned from all our homes. It was considered lucky for a cat to sleep on one of our parochial school uniforms. In the carriage house where Madeline once stored her tattered scripts, and where Aunt Kate now lived, a ghost light burned in an upper window, a forty-watt bulb in a floor lamp without a shade. Our attics were full of ruined costumes, tattered moth's-wings of burned velvet and lace that had been court gowns; crinolines reduced to hoops of whalebone; black satin disks that, when smacked upon a cousin's unsuspecting head, burgeoned into top hats; lady's gloves that still smelled like the ladies who had last worn them; sinister puppets and jointed dolls used as models for the wardrobe mistress; old photos of Fairhaven, the island in Maine where Madeline had kept a summer home.

But most of the photographs of Madeline had ended up in Aunt Kate's house. Faded silver-print and sepia images, water damaged or foxed with mold. Still, you could see how striking she'd been, with large, very pale eyes that looked ghostly in black-and-white, a high forehead and thick dark hair, melancholy mouth, and the faintest constellation of freckles across her apple cheeks. She was piquant rather than pretty; yet there was also something unsettling in her looks, though maybe that was just the old-fashioned photography. All the pictures seemed slightly out of focus.

And I could never imagine her eyes having a color. Were they blue? Gray? Green?

They looked like ice. I couldn't imagine her ever crying.

Fey, said Aunt Kate whenever she mentioned her. A word I didn't understand, especially when she added, "You look like her, Maddy."

Because I was ugly. Really ugly; everyone thought so. Crooked buckteeth and glasses, upturned nose, bad skin. The grown-ups called me Skinny Wretch—fondly, but still. Only Aunt Kate would look at me and shake her head, sitting at her dressing table surrounded by her beautiful clothes, Pucci dresses, Betsey Johnson shifts, Yves Saint Laurent blouses transparent as a screen door. On her right hand she wore a ring that had belonged to my great-grandmother, with an emerald roughly the shape and size of a cat's eye.

"You're beautiful, Maddy. Those legs? Just you wait. And when your braces come off? And the glasses? *Glamorous.* You're going to be so *glamorous*—"

And she'd give me a special bar of soap from France, or astringent ointment from London that smelled like coal smoke. "Just you wait."

At my age, my great-grandmother was already beautiful. By the time she was sixteen, she was famous. As a girl, Madeline created unforgettable portrayals of Rosalind, Juliet, Titania, Perdita, and especially Viola, as well as less memorable turns in works like *Storming Castle Dora* and *The Blue-Footed Boy.*

"Unforgettable." That was the word attached to Madeline throughout her career, in every torn clipping I ever read, every review of every performance, every stagy publicity photo that appeared as ancient and remote to me as a stone tablet. Madeline's Unforgettable Cleopatra. Her Unforgettable Viola. Her Unforgettable Series of Unforgettable Triumphs, Never to Be Forgotten.

Only, of course, it's all forgotten now. It was all forgotten then, since none of our parents had ever known Madeline as anything but a fractious old woman holed up in Fairview, her decaying Yonkers mansion. Even in her dotage she was too self-absorbed to pay much attention to her own five children, let alone her grandchildren.

But she'd made a good marriage to a wealthy developer named Rosco O'Meara, a man who anticipated the late-twentieth-century vogue for gated communities by nearly a century. They had five children, all of whom retained Madeline's maiden name. Almost unheard-of at the time, but Madeline belonged to a dynasty, and she was determined it would live on. Her twin brothers, also noted thespians, died of misadventure and left no children. She was the last of her line.

In the early 1900s, Rosco built Arden Terrace, a speculative venture consisting of a score of expansive Shingle-style and Tudor and Gothic homes, along with carriage houses, guesthouses, and various outbuildings, in a huge cul-de-sac overlooking the Hudson River. Artists flocked there from the city—North Yonkers was an exurb in those days, with fields and woodlands and bald eagles nesting along the river—and Arden Terrace became an enclave of successful writers and actors and editors, doctors and lawyers and a stockbroker.

Lovely and otherworldly as Arden Terrace was, it was also vulnerable. When the stock market crashed in 1929, no fewer than seven residents killed themselves, including Madeline's husband. Not, however, Madeline, who seemed to have absorbed the cumulative resilience and resourcefulness of all those plucky heroines she'd once played (her sole substantial flop was as Juliet) and who during the Depression bought up, one by one, all the houses surrounding her own. Her children ended up living in those homes, like hermit crabs scuttling into empty shells; and then *their* children, Madeline's grandchildren; and finally my own generation of kids.

By which time Arden Terrace resembled some mad architectural folly spread out across one of the more desirable pieces of real estate in the city. Year after year, the Hudson River moved slowly, far below the turrets and balconies of our ersatz fortress; the tulip trees shed their yellow leaves; and snow covered the slate roofs of the carriage houses and guest cottages where the oldest Tierneys now lived. When summer came, the cul-de-sac was taken over by an occupying army of children in Keds and dungarees and striped shirts from John Wanamaker. Rock and roll blared from upstairs bedrooms, while a legion of mothers and aunts and grandmothers sat on Fairview's immense porch, talking and smoking and drinking whiskey sours as they watched the sun set over the Palisades.

Rogan's father and mine grew up in Fairview, along with their sisters. Later, Rogan's father inherited the mansion—he was the older twin by twelve minutes—and Rogan grew up there. My father moved into the house across the street, a less grand Queen Anne home that still had five bathrooms, exorbitant for the time, and six bedrooms.

That was where I grew up. Though the truth was, I spent as much time at Rogan's home as my own, and nearly as much time where our other cousins lived. During the day we all attended St. Brendan's School, several blocks away, up a winding hill shaded by old apartment buildings and elm trees, all now long gone. Every afternoon we raced home and changed from our uniforms into what were then called play clothes—a misnomer, since our after-school activities were more like the extended rehearsal for a street-theater production of *Lord of the Flies*. We moved from house to house to house like invading army ants. We devoured everything we could find, terrorized the youngest children, raided toy chests and attics, crowded into basement rec rooms to watch *Star Trek* and *Superman,* stole each other's record albums and baseball cards and Barbie clothes, gave too much food to goldfish and dogs that were not our own—all until we were driven back outside by irate adults.

Whereupon we'd move next door, or across the road, or down to the woods overlooking the river, and the whole cycle would begin again.

And Rogan?

There was never a time when I did not know Rogan.

We were the youngest in our generation of cousins. As the youngest girl, I wasn't coddled; mostly tolerated by my sisters and ignored by our parents.

But as the youngest boy, Rogan was bullied and beaten and tormented, relentlessly, cruelly; almost absently.

"Why?" I once demanded of Rogan's brother Michael. I'd jumped onto him from a first-floor balcony at my house when I saw him pounding Rogan on the lawn below. Michael grabbed me and tossed me onto the early-spring grass as though I were a burr that had stuck to him, and not a gangly fourteen-year-old girl with glasses. Rogan ran off, his face crimson with tears. I stumbled to my feet and shouted at Michael, "Why can't you just leave him alone?"

"What?" Michael looked at me, his blue eyes grave with astonishment. I might have asked him why we had to eat or drink or attend Mass on Sundays. "Because he'd be *spoiled.*"

Spoiled. It was the worst thing you could be. Only children were spoiled, not that we knew any. Aunt Kate, who'd never married and who had kept her looks, along with a pied-à-terre in Greenwich Village—she was spoiled. Younger siblings by definition were spoiled, since in some obscure way they'd spoiled the paradise occupied by their older brothers and sisters, simply by being born.

So it went without saying that Rogan and I were in danger of being the most spoiled of all. What made it worse was that Rogan had trouble at school. We were in the same class. He was smart but fidgety, the nuns would yell at him for daydreaming, he couldn't focus on homework.

I helped him, reading books out loud, the two of us taking turns; not just schoolbooks but the books we read for fun. In eighth grade that year we'd read *Macbeth*, and at home Rogan and I did all the different parts, Rogan the men, me the women.

And this, too, was considered some obscure betrayal by our brothers and sisters. Since our parents couldn't be trusted to do anything, it was up to our siblings and cousins to make sure we didn't end up flouncing along North Broadway in our underwear, disgracing the rest of the clan. I had my share of black eyes and bruises, but most of these came from defending Rogan. I can see now that much of what he endured was probably the result of rampant, if unspoken, homophobia in a large family of boys and the larger tribe of male cousins. Gays weren't invented yet, not in North Yonkers anyway. You were a guy, or you were a faggot.

The irony, of course, was that Rogan wasn't gay. He was in love with me, as I was with him.

And that was maybe the only thing worse than being gay.

No one had ever heard of DNA back then, not in my family

anyway, and our grasp of genetics was practically nonexistent. But, because our fathers were identical twins, their children had all been told—warned—that we were closer than the other cousins.

"More like stepchildren," said Aunt Dita.

"Half-brothers and -sisters," my mother corrected her.

"Kissing cousins," said Aunt Roz. That would be the cue for everyone to cast a cold eye upon Rogan and me.

Now I waited till Michael turned to look for his brother, then I darted up behind him and kicked him squarely in the back of the knee. Michael shouted in pain and crumpled to the grass, his arm lashing out to grab me.

But I was already gone.

I knew where Rogan was—beneath Fairview. A labyrinth of storerooms, root cellars, garden rooms, and disused workshops tunneled under my great-grandmother's house. Once, they'd been tended by a small army of servants and gardeners. For the last fifty years, they'd pretty much fallen into decay. All the doors and stairways that led to the upper house had been boarded up.

Now, the only entrance was behind a thick curtain of wisteria that hung from the great porch above. You had to know where it was—a gap in the wooden trellis that peeled from the house like a scab from a wound. The wisteria looked beautiful, blade-shaped leaves and clusters of blossoms like grapes made of blue tissue. But the flowers smelled horrible, like rotting meat, and they drew clouds of greenflies and bluebottles.

Rogan wasn't afraid of the flies and wisteria. He wasn't afraid of anything.

But I was. I took a deep breath and pinched my nose, closed my eyes and shoved aside the moving tangle of leaves, and ducked inside.

Beneath the porch, it was dim and cool and smelled of earth and old paint. A harlequin pattern of sunlight filtered through the trellis, pied with the shadows of leaves and vines. There were clay pots and rusted garden tools underfoot; also large black beetles and yellow- or blue-spotted salamanders that looked like lost toys. There were brown recluse spiders, too, which various elderly aunts claimed had caused the deaths of careless servants in an earlier day; cave crickets; and, flanking the small raised doorway that led into a dark anteroom, a half dozen plaster leprechauns that my grandfather had brought back from one of his yearly trips to Connemara. The leprechauns were the size of small children, and painted in too-bright colors— bottle-green jackets, scarlet caps, yellow belt buckles. Most of the paint had gone from their faces, which gave them the eerie look of grave monuments.

I was afraid of them, too.

Rogan knew that. And so he waited, as always, squatting inside the doorway with one hand already outstretched to pull me up beside him. I flapped my hand at the ground, scattering invisible bugs, then sat.

"Thanks," said Rogan.

He reached into a niche between two wallboards where we kept a candle in a blue glass holder and a box of matches, lit the candle, and set it back in the wall. The unsteady light washed over him and I stared, as always; unembarrassed because we were alone, and it was dark. And it was Rogan.

He was so beautiful. I never understood why it wasn't spoken: that he was the most beautiful boy you had ever seen. Or maybe it was only me who felt that. The Tierneys were all tall, and our hair was brown or fair or tawny, and we all had deep-blue eyes. There hadn't been a Tierney with anything but blue eyes in five hundred years, my father said. All of the Tierney boys were handsome in a bluff, clean-shaven Hyannisport way, and most of the girls were pretty.

Rogan looked like he'd fallen from a painting.

He was tall like the rest of us, with long legs, long arms, square sturdy hands. His hair was reddish-gold, fine as a baby's hair, and he grew it as long as he could until his father dragged him to the barber up in Getty Square. He had high cheekbones in a feline face—not like a house cat's; more a cougar or lynx, something strong and furtive and quick. His nose was like mine, although it had been broken more than once. His mouth was wide and surprisingly delicate, the only thing about him that might have seemed girlish. Until he smiled, and showed narrow white teeth that were also like an animal's. He had huge, deep-set eyes—wary eyes, which made it slightly alarming when he suddenly turned them on you—and they weren't Tierney blue but a true aquamarine, the palest blue-green, changeable as seawater in sunlight or cloud.

But the most striking thing about him was the way he moved. Gracefully—sensually, I would have said if I were older—but also with this strange lightness, almost an unease; as though he had trouble getting his footing. His arms moved as if drawing patterns in the air; he'd tilt his head sometimes like he heard something. Even his furtive gaze wasn't sly but oddly watchful.

Yet it wasn't a vigilance that protected him from his brothers or his father, and it was also completely unconscious—I knew because I watched him constantly, had been watching him for as long as I could remember, and maybe for longer.

Once I eavesdropped, unseen, as Aunt Kate and my mother discussed him. The two of them didn't like each other: my mother was suspicious of her sister-in-law's oddly ageless beauty, her chic black gamine hair and expensive clothes, and, it was whispered, her wealthy lovers.

"Fey," Aunt Kate said. She twisted her emerald ring as though it hurt her finger. "Rogan's fey." My mother must have made a face, because Aunt Kate went on, annoyed. "That's *not* what it means."

I heard my mother draw on her cigarette. "All I can say is, if I ever had a red-headed child, I'd strangle it."

Now, watching Rogan, all I wanted to do was touch him. Instead I clutched my own skinny thighs and looked at him sideways, while he held up the match and watched it burn to his fingertips. Finally he tossed the match aside.

"Listen," he said.

I cocked my head. "I don't hear anything."

"No, idiot—listen to *me*. My voice. Listen to me talking. Talking talking talking. Hear it?"

I did. "Wow," I said. "It broke!"

"Yeah. And listen to *this*—"

He put his hands on his knees and leaned forward, his face jutting into the darkness until I could no longer see it. He began to sing.

"When all beside a vigil keep,
The West's asleep, the West's asleep . . ."

My flesh crawled. I knew the song from one of my father's Clancy Brothers records. "The West's Awake."

"And long a brave and haughty race
Honoured and sentinelled the place.
Sing, Oh! not e'en their sons' disgrace
Can quite destroy their glory's trace . . ."

I had never heard it sung like this. I had never heard *anything* sung like this, or heard a guy's voice remotely sound like this. It wasn't even singing; more a sustained wail, Rogan's mouth somehow shaping words that seemed to claw against the voice that formed them. He was *keening*, in a tenor so pure and wild and primal that it didn't even sound like music: it was like being burned by a song. It was like hearing something die.

"But hark! a voice like thunder spake,
The West's awake! The West's awake . . ."

His voice rose to a falsetto, then fell. It held the last notes for so long that I couldn't tell when they faded into an echo, until the echo itself dropped into silence and Rogan sank back into the half-light beside me.

"Holy cow." I was crying—when had I started to cry?—not just my face wet but my hands, my shirt, my jeans. "Rogan, that—"

I stopped. His chin was tucked against his chest, his hands clutching his head as he rocked back and forth, mouth bared in a grimace as he moaned something over and over again, words I couldn't understand. I didn't even know if they *were* words. He looked ghastly, unearthly; like a picture I had once seen of a body trapped in a lava flow. I stared, too terrified to move, until he turned toward me and I saw his eyes, his own face streaked with tears; and suddenly I understood what he was saying—

"I made that—I made that—I made that—"

I grabbed him, hugging him to my skinny chest as we both began to laugh hysterically.

"That was me!" He almost shrieked, and I covered his mouth with my hand, still laughing. "That was *me!*"

"Shut up! Rogan, shhh—"

He bit my finger. I yelped and snatched my hand back, then fell on him. He held me so hard I punched him.

"You're choking me!"

He relaxed his hold. I rubbed my face against his shirt to dry my tears, then pressed my fist against his chest. His heart pounded so hard it was like another fist hammered inside him and I splayed my fingers, imagining I could hold it, like a baseball, or a stone. He smelled as he always did, of detergent and sweat, his mother's Chanel No. 5, and dirt and chalk dust.

But he smelled of something else, too. He smelled the way his brothers did, and my older boy cousins; their tree-house smell, sweetish and rank, slightly ammoniacal; at once green and earthen. No one had told me what that smell was, and nobody ever would.

But I knew.

"Maddy," he whispered.

He ran his finger along my chapped lips, then lightly tapped the wires of my braces. I took off my glasses as he tilted his head and brought his mouth close, rubbing his lips across mine. His breath was warm and sour. I stroked his hair, tentatively, drew my hand down to cup his ear then touched his cheek, the line of his jaw. He'd always felt like me, smooth and clean. I had never noticed hair on his face but I felt it now, his skin damp and slightly abraded, like touching a cat's tongue. He angled himself so that he was on top of me and gently pushed me down, so that we were lying face-to-face.

We stayed like that forever, breathing, sometimes moving. I felt as though my clothes had disappeared, and my skin; as though my bones had uncurled like ferns to twine with his. Finally he stirred and touched my face.

"Where are your glasses?"

We sat up. The candle had burned out. The dark underground room felt warmer than it had earlier, and it no longer smelled like dirt and earthworms. It smelled like Rogan. It smelled like us.

"It will all be different now," he said. His tone absent, as though reciting something he only half remembered. "Will you help me with that stuff for math?"

"Sure," I said, and scrambled after him to head back outside.

❖ ❖ ❖

ROGAN WAS RIGHT: IT WAS DIFFERENT. NOT ALL AT once, and not immediately.

But the world changed, everything about us changed. Everything about me, certainly.

The school year ended. It was the summer before high school. Early in July my braces came off. After that I refused to get my hair cut in the ghastly pixie cut I'd had since I was two years old. The stuff Aunt Kate gave me for my skin began to work. My face cleared up.

And I started to wean myself from my glasses, using them only to read, or when my parents were around. The rest of the time I kept them in an ugly orange case in my pocket, until the day that I forgot the case in my room.

"Maddy." My mother frowned when she saw me at breakfast. "Where are your glasses? You didn't lose them?"

I took a deep breath. "I don't need them anymore."

My mother made the face she made at dinner when someone said they weren't hungry.

"I really don't," I said quickly. "I can read fine. Aunt Kate said you should take me to see Dr. Gordon and he'll tell you."

"Aunt Kate." My mother glowered. But she did take me to see Dr. Gordon.

And it was true, Dr. Gordon said I didn't need my glasses. Someday I would, when I was older, but for now, as long as I didn't get headaches, I could do without them.

"Hooray!" said Rogan. He had grown two more inches, and was now a full head taller than me. "You look a *lot* better."

Aunt Kate regarded me more measuringly.

"I'll take you to my salon." She rubbed the ends of my hair between her fingers and grimaced. "Alain will know what to do about this."

The next time she went into the city, I went with her. My hair was trimmed, not cut, by Alain, a man who wore one chandelier earring and motorcycle boots.

"Beautiful eyes," he said. He glanced at my aunt in the mirror. "How old?"

"She'll be fifteen in October."

"Ohhhh." He smiled at me and arched his eyebrows rakishly. "You're in high school!"

"In the fall," I said.

He nodded, bending to snip my bangs. "Boyfriend?"

I looked up to see Aunt Kate staring back at me from the mirror, the blue Tierney eyes brilliant and faintly threatening in that elegant, ageless face.

"No," she said.

When Alain was finished, Aunt Kate paid him, then took me to lunch at O'Neals' Baloon.

"Good," she said. She watched approvingly as I ate my hot fudge sundae. "This will grow out nicely, Maddy. You look very glamorous."

Rogan had changed as well. He wasn't just taller—his voice had grown, too. At night I'd listen as he stepped onto the tiny balcony outside his room and sang "Wild Horses" in that eerie keening tenor. When he stopped, we'd double over laughing as all the Tierney dogs began to howl, followed by a chorus of angry grown-ups yelling at them to shut up.

In July Rogan joined the choir at St. Brendan's. Not the children's choir, which was all girls—not me, I couldn't sing—but the grown-up choir, which sang at ten thirty High Mass. Our fathers attended Mass on Saturday afternoon so they could play golf on Sunday morning. Our mothers and siblings went to twelve o'clock Mass on Sunday, for those laggards who slept late. Aunt Kate only went at Christmas and Easter.

But I'd walk up with Rogan and sit in the middle of the church (High Mass was never crowded) and listen, bewitched, as his voice soared through the vaulted space, chanting the *Kyrie* and *Te Deum* and *Gloria in excelsis*. It made my flesh crawl. Not just me: I could see other members of the congregation shift uncomfortably in their pews, Tierney great-uncles and -aunts and the Connells' grandparents all staring fixedly at their missalettes until old Monsignor Burke sang the Recessional in his quavering voice, and the Mass was ended.

Only Mrs. Rossi, our diminutive school secretary, seemed to feel as I did. Once she waited with me outside the church for Rogan to come down from the choir loft.

"That was so beautiful, Rogan," she whispered as the rest of the congregation hurried to their cars. "You should be singing at St. Patrick's Cathedral."

Rogan waited till she left, then made a face.

"Another church? Screw that," he said, and we walked home.

Back on Arden Terrace, we hung out with kids from school who came down from Mile Square Road. Our siblings and cousins were all in high school now, or college. One of Aunt Trixie's boys had joined the military. My oldest sister, Brigid, was engaged. Occasion-ally Michael would pound Rogan, or try to, but Rogan was bigger now. After a while Michael lost interest in the sport and, concomi-tantly, in Rogan himself. We weren't watched as closely as we once were. When our parents went out to dinner at the club, Rogan and I were left alone.

Or sort of alone. My sisters, perversely, paid more attention to me now than when I was younger; a chilly feminine vigilance to ensure I did nothing to embarrass them, especially with Rogan.

So he and I would engineer games of hide-and-seek with the kids from Mile Square Road, and *then* disappear. We'd hide beneath the porch at Fairview, and forgo the candle to lie in the dark with Rogan on top of me. We'd hold each other and pretend we'd been shipwrecked.

"I can't breathe," Rogan would whisper as he clutched me. Some-times he'd pinch my nostrils shut. "You can't breathe, your mouth is filled with water . . ."

We knew we weren't drowning. We knew what we were doing, even though I never quite had a word for it, Rogan's smell and breath and our hearts hammering as we moved, the raw feel of my groin rubbed beneath layers of cotton and denim. Afterward we'd lie on the cold earth and talk and listen to the voices of the others outside as they looked for us, excited then laughing then irritated then bored and finally, as the summer wore toward fall, angry and obdurate. The day came when Rogan called and asked Ookie Connell to come over. I could tell by Rogan's face that the answer was no, and when he put the phone down he shrugged.

"What?" I asked.

"He says if we have a baby it'll be retarded."

In September we started high school. The only two classes we had together were English and Latin. For the latter, Sister Mary Clark made a point of separating us.

"But I help him," I protested. "I help him concentrate."

"I'm sure you do." Sister Mark Clark had taught two generations of Tierneys. She liked my sisters, and she liked me. She was a bony, raw-faced woman who still wore a habit and laughed a lot, though her eyes were long and bright as a knife. "Rogan needs to concentrate by himself. He can't rely on you, Madeline. He has to do his own work."

"He does! He—"

She grabbed my elbow and pinched it hard. "I want you over here."

She guided me to the other side of the classroom. I sat, scowling, as Sister Mary Clark started back across the room. Abruptly she stopped and turned to me. Her eyes narrowed.

"Madeline, where are your glasses?"

I stared back. "I don't need them anymore."

She looked at me, then at Rogan watching me from the other side of the room. He flushed, and her gaze hardened.

"Do not peer too close," she said, deliberately misquoting Pindar. "Everyone, get out yesterday's homework."

A few weeks later we were walking home from school. It was the end of September, a Friday afternoon. Rogan wore a battered fatigue coat over his uniform; I wore his brown corduroy jacket, too big for me. Several other kids from school walked near us. Their voices dropped as they passed. Ookie Connell said something I couldn't hear, and the others laughed.

"I quit the choir," Rogan said as we started down the hill toward Arden Terrace, walking along the curb so we could kick through drifts of leaves.

"How come?"

"Old Mrs. Connell complained." He shook his head, his red-gold hair spilling to his collar. "She said my singing distracted her."

I laughed. "Distracted! Can she even hear you?"

But Rogan didn't smile.

"She's a bitch." He glanced back to make sure the others were gone, then leaned down to touch his head to mine. "This friend of Michael's, Derek, he was over last night. He's in a band. He told me I should come hear them. He said maybe I could sing with them sometime."

"Really?" I smiled, but felt a twinge of unease. I didn't recognize it as jealousy. "Where do they play?"

"I dunno. Someplace in Ardsley. Listen, I want to show you something. When you come over. I found a place."

A place. I knew what that meant. When summer ended, our spot beneath the porch grew cold and overrun with beetles. Field mice sought shelter against the coming winter, and hibernating bats.

"The isle is sinking into the ice," I'd warned Rogan as we lay there in the chilly dark. "We must seek safe harbor, or drown."

"There is no safe harbor," he'd said, and kissed me till I couldn't breathe.

Now I slowed to look at him. The worn fatigue coat made him seem older—a beautiful stranger, like someone on an album cover. His hair was the same color as the maple leaves, his cheeks were reddened from the cold. His eerie eyes caught the cloudless sweep of sky and glowed a startling, mineral blue.

"Is it a good place?" I asked.

Rogan grinned. "It's a *great* place. Wait'll you see it."

When we reached Arden Terrace I went home and changed. My sisters were out. My mother had taken a job in the women's department at Wanamaker's and wouldn't be home till dinnertime. I grabbed my Latin text and went across the street to Rogan's house, to pretend to do homework.

Rogan's father, like mine, was a successful stockbroker, but he always said there wasn't enough money in the world to maintain Fairview. Everywhere shingles were missing. Paint flaked from the balconies on the upper floors. The great porch sagged where it overlooked the Hudson, its wicker furniture unsprung and its balustrades devoured by carpenter ants.

Inside, the house was cold and smelled of stale cigarette smoke and dust. Rogan's mother, too, had taken a job. Autumn leaves had blown across the antique Caucasian carpets. There were semicircles of ash in front of the fireplaces; in the kitchen and bathrooms, sinks bore serpentine trails of rust beneath their faucets.

But on the third floor, where Rogan slept, little had changed. Adults ventured there seldom, chiefly to complain or enact justice: it had the austere air of benign neglect associated with a lakeside home in the off-season. Rogan's brothers Michael and Thomas had the two bedrooms overlooking the front of the house. As usual, they were off with their girlfriends. Rogan stood on the landing, waiting for me.

"Greetings, fair Amazon." He swept out his arm in welcome. "Come into the parlor."

Once his room had been the nursery. It was a wide, sunlit space that occupied nearly half of the third floor, with a row of windows that looked straight across the river, though when you gazed out you mostly saw unbroken sky. It should have seemed cheerful and bright.

Instead, the room felt empty and exposed, even desolate. Temporary quarters, despite Rogan's having lived there his entire life. A sink stood in one corner, an institutional relic of nursery life, and next to it the door that opened onto a tiny morning balcony, big enough for just one person. There were alcoves filled with moldering books and Samuel French scripts that had been defaced by mice. Rag rugs covered the floor. A creepy archaeology of wallpaper peeled in layers from the walls—fox hunters, lurid pink lilacs, Humpty Dumpty.

A bunged-up kitchen table served as desk, and there were two spindly chairs that had been painted meat-red. Beneath the windows stood a very beautiful hand-carved cradle, rumored to have belonged to one of Madeline's twin brothers. Rogan used it as a hamper. A wooden hatbox hid his cigarettes. In the middle of the room was an immense theatrical trunk, its brass fittings black with age, where he kept his clothes. You could just make out the name stenciled on its top in faint white letters.

MADELINE ARMIN TIERNEY

I used to wonder why the trunk was here, rather than in Aunt Kate's carriage house. That was until Rogan and I attempted to move it. It wouldn't budge, not even when we enlisted Michael's help.

"Jesus, what's in there? Rocks?" Michael complained, wiping sweat from his lip.

"Uh-uh. Just this—"

Rogan tossed a pair of socks at him. The two ended up scuffling on the floor, until my uncle pounded upstairs and cracked their heads together. Before he went back down he gave the trunk a baleful glance, then looked darkly at Rogan.

"Next time it'll be *you* in there," he said.

Rogan slept in a wrought-iron bed against one wall. There was a bookshelf beside it, and next to that a small door that opened into a long, low, paneled space that was half closet, half attic. It was crammed with boxes of toy machine guns and water pistols, old Halloween noisemakers and masks, crepe-paper streamers and piles of *The Saturday Evening Post*, tinsel garland, and compacts of greasepaint and rouge. Glitter had sifted over everything, like silver dust. It smelled like Christmas, of cloves and balsam.

"Come here, Maddy." Rogan took my hand and drew me to him. "Come and see . . ."

He stepped to the wall, opened the door to the little attic, and ducked inside, stooping so he wouldn't graze his head against the ceiling. I followed.

"Wait—stay there for a minute," he said. Carefully he stepped between cartons of wigs and old magazines, until he reached the end of the narrow space. He pulled out a flashlight and switched it on, then gestured at the door behind me. "Close that, then come over here. Try not to knock anything over."

I shut the door and joined him in the back of the room. "What is it?"

We stood side by side, backs bent, between boxes of Shiny Brite Christmas ornaments. Directly in front of us, more cartons were stacked against the wall.

"Take this," Rogan commanded. He handed me the flashlight, then knelt. Very gingerly he began to pull the pile of boxes toward him, wedging himself against the stack so that they moved as one and didn't topple over. "Now look. Do you see it?"

He leaned back and shone the flashlight on the wall.

Where the boxes had been was another door. Barely three feet high and not as wide, with a simple latch and hinges that had darkened to the same oaky color as the walls.

"Wow," I breathed. "How'd you find it?"

"Just poking around the other night. There's stuff in here, I swear no one's touched it since Madeline died." Rogan grinned. "No one knows about it but us. Here—"

He undid the latch and pulled the door open, took the flashlight and shone it inside, then motioned at me.

"Go in," he urged. "I fixed it up. Go on, I'm right behind you."

I squatted, got onto my hands and knees, and crawled inside. I could see nothing clearly, but a moment later Rogan's head bumped against me.

"Keep going," he said. "Once you get all the way in you can kneel; just watch your head. But it's bigger than you think."

I laughed in delight, my heart beating fast, and crawled into the near-darkness. Something soft was under me; the flashlight moved wildly as Rogan turned and pulled the door closed behind us. I heard the soft *thhkkk* of a match being struck, and then Rogan lit a candle and set it into a blue glass he'd stolen from church.

"That's not safe," I said.

Rogan snorted and turned off the flashlight.

"Voilà," he said.

We were in a passage under the eaves. To one side, the ceiling slanted down to the floor. On the other side was a fretwork of wood and plaster lath. The wavering blue candlelight made it seem as though this wall was snow covered and moonlit. A neat pallet of Hudson Bay blankets lay on the floor, along with an ashtray and a pack of cigarettes.

Also several books, including the copy of *Tales from Shakespeare* that had once been Madeline's but which I had claimed years before, only to have it disappear.

"Hey!" I grabbed the book and stared at the cover in disbelief, then smacked Rogan with it. "You stole this!"

"Yeah, but I gave it back." He flopped onto the blankets. "What do you think?"

"It's amazing." I lay beside him and stared at the ceiling. "It's like being in a boat."

"That's right." He turned toward me. "It's the boat that saved us from drowning."

He kissed me, his mouth so much bigger than mine, and his hands; everything. When I grasped his shoulders it was like grabbing onto a ladder: I clambered on top of him and he slipped his hands beneath my flannel shirt.

"It's warm here," he whispered. "We can be warm."

We took our shirts off, and for the first time drew ourselves together skin to skin, breast to breast. His flesh was as white and smooth as my own, all but hairless; his nipples small and flat above the long hollow of his waist and his hip bone's sharp rise; his mouth bittersweet with nicotine and toothpaste. Everywhere I touched him was like finding myself in the dark. Rogan's hands moved where mine would move. His murmurs echoed my own. The space around us was another, warmer skin, its reek of sex and sweat cut with the chalky scent of plaster and that intense, oddly evanescent balsam smell. We kept our jeans on, striving together until first Rogan came and then I did, straddling his thigh.

Afterward we lay entwined. Small moons quivered all around us, blue and gold and silver, as the candle guttered in its glass.

"Shhh," I said, though neither of us had spoken. "Listen." I pressed my hand on Rogan's mouth and whispered, "Do you hear?"

"Mice," said Rogan. "They're everywhere."

"That's not mice."

From behind the wall came a faint tapping. Not scrabbling or scratching; more rhythmic. I sat up, my sweat cooling, and cocked my head.

"It's there." I touched the wall with the flat of my hand—warily, as though it might burn me. "Can't you hear it?"

It sounded like drumming fingernails. Or sleet, if sleet could fall inside a house.

Yet the sky had been cloudless.

Rogan yawned. "It's mice, Maddy."

The thought of mice made my bare flesh prickle. I snatched up my flannel shirt and started to pull it on.

"Hey!" Rogan tugged my sleeve. "Don't do that! I was looking."

"I'm cold. Well, not cold, but I don't want mice crawling on me."

"How about *this?*"

He pulled me toward him. I smacked him, not hard, and pretended to struggle. He pinned me to the floor, I kicked at the blankets as he laughed and tickled me.

"Rogan! Don't—"

I kicked again. My aim went wild and my foot connected with the wall. I felt the wood buckle.

Then, alarmingly, the wall pushed back.

"Shit." With all my strength I pushed Rogan away. "Damn it, look. I broke something."

One of the wood panels had come loose and fallen onto the blankets, leaving a gap as wide as my hand. I nudged the board with my foot, then froze.

From inside the wall, light glimmered. Neither cold blue candle-flame nor an electric bulb; more like starlight, fractured and wavering yet also warm, as though embers had rained from the rafters. For an instant the rhythmic tapping fell silent. Then it started up again, louder now that the wall had been breached.

And I could hear something else besides that soft strange pattering—a susurrus, sweet and high-pitched, like the sound that hunting swallows made in the twilight above Fairview's lawns. I leaned, breathless, toward the opening. Rogan did the same. His arm circled me as our faces drew within inches of the gap.

"Oh, Maddy," he breathed. "Oh, Maddy, look."

Inside the wall was a toy theater, made of folded paper and gilt cardboard and scraps of brocade and lace. Curtains of scarlet tissue shrouded the proscenium. The stage floor was mottled yellow and green, as though to suggest a field starred with flowers. Thumbnail-sized masks of Comedy and Tragedy hung from the proscenium arch, beneath a frieze of Muses that looked as though it had been painted with a single hair. Columns no bigger than a pencil rose to either side, and a dizzyingly intricate arrangement of trompe l'oeil cutouts and folded paper walls and arches made it seem as though the stage receded endlessly, into topiary gardens and ruined statuary, a fallen tower and snow-peaked mountains and, most distant of all, a beach of golden sand with a ruined ship silhouetted against a wintry sun. A row of tiny footlights burned at the edge of the apron, each light the size of a glowing match-head, and there were loops of colored string that hung from the flies, so the curtains could be raised and flats or scrims lowered.

There was even an orchestra pit.

But no orchestra. No actors or stage manager or director.

And no audience, save for Rogan and me. We craned our necks, trying to see it all.

We couldn't. The opening was too small.

And the toy theater, tiny as it was, was too big. Rogan shook his head and gazed at me questioningly.

"Mice," I said.

We both started laughing, our voices edging into hysteria. Rogan finally drew a shuddering breath and wiped his eyes. "How the hell did they get that in there?"

"Jesus, I have no idea." I rubbed my neck. "*Who* put it there? That's what I want to know."

"Maybe they just stuck it inside. Or, you know, built it in pieces then assembled it."

I gave him a dubious look. "How?"

"I dunno. How do they put ships in bottles? Maybe it was like that."

We both turned and peered back inside. The eerie rustling and tapping continued unabated, though nothing moved save the shadows cast by the diminutive footlights.

"There's lights in there," I said flatly. "Those little lights? How come it doesn't burn down? *Who lit them?*"

Abruptly I felt sick. Rogan grew pale. He bit his lip, then reached to thrust his hand through the opening.

"Don't!" I stopped him, gasping, and shook my head. "Don't."

"Why not?" demanded Rogan. But he sat up, crossed his arms, and stared at me. "Is it—"

"I don't know what it is. But."

I grabbed the fallen board and started to angle it back into place, then hesitated. Without looking at each other, we lowered our heads once more.

It was all still there, the picture-frame proscenium and paint-spattered floor, gilt-and-cardboard mountains and tissue curtains and rows of paper columns stretching to an impossible distance beneath an impossible sunrise. For a long time we gazed at it, our cheeks touching, until finally I drew away.

"We should go." I felt a sudden pang. "If someone found it . . ."

We looked at each other, our hair tangled, Rogan still shirtless. He nodded.

Silently I replaced the panel, making certain we could remove it next time. Rogan blew out the candle and switched on his flashlight. We dressed; I grabbed my copy of *Tales from Shakespeare*, and we crept into the attic storeroom. I helped Rogan move the stacked boxes back into place against the wall, then followed him into his bedroom.

We didn't talk about what we had seen. I felt exalted but also subdued, near tears. Rogan went to the window and stared at the sky, twilit now, the sun a red disk above the Palisades and a shimmering strand of lights poised between the hill where Fairview stood and the nebulous glow of Manhattan, ten miles downriver.

"It looks so far away," he said at last.

I crossed to stand beside him. "It's not, really."

For a few minutes we remained there, watching until the sun disappeared behind the cliffs and the sky darkened to indigo. From a room below a television droned. I could smell roasting chicken and hear Michael talking on the phone. Rogan looked at me and smiled ruefully.

"Latin?" he asked.

We got our textbooks and went downstairs.

❖ ❖ ❖

I STAYED FOR DINNER THAT NIGHT. MICHAEL WAS there—he was a high school senior that fall—and Thomas, who commuted to his first year at Fordham. And Aunt Pat, who'd arrived home from her job at Gimbels to get the chicken and potatoes in the oven.

She was slight and briskly cheerful, her fair hair streaked with gray, her skin taut and lined from smoking.

"Your mom says you're doing well with all your classes," she said as she handed me the string beans.

"Yeah, pretty well, I guess."

"Not like Knucklehead here." She looked fondly at her youngest son. "See if you can get it to rub off on him, will you, Maddy?"

Michael made a crude face. "That shouldn't be too hard."

Rogan kicked him under the table. "You—"

Just then we all heard the front door open. Aunt Pat raised her eyebrows but said nothing. The rest of us straightened in our chairs, even Thomas, who had grown a beard when he started college and had yet to shave it. I paid great interest to my chicken, as I listened to the familiar sound of a briefcase being dropped, the door to the hall closet opening and closing, and then my uncle Richard's tread across the foyer and into the dining room, a heavier echo of my own father's footsteps.

"Hello, everyone."

It was a big doorway, but my uncle filled it. Neither he nor my father was particularly tall. Both scanted six feet, both were wiry though strongly built, broad-shouldered, long-legged, with light-brown hair barely thinning from their foreheads.

But, as the older twin, my uncle seemed to have absorbed the greater psychic mass. He was a bit grayer than my father, more worn about the face—like Aunt Pat, he was a heavy smoker—and more choleric. Seeing both twins in a crowded room, you might be hard put at first to tell them apart.

But inevitably, your gaze would be drawn to my uncle. Even in daylight he appeared to stand half-shadowed, and no matter how animated he was, you were always conscious of something waiting, a coiled anticipation. It was only as I grew older that I realized this sense of expectation didn't come from my uncle himself. It emanated from his children. Being in a room with his sons was like standing in a pen crammed with nervous horses. Their fear was palpable, and their mute hatred; their love.

The older boys all resembled him. Only Rogan was different, with his flaming hair and uncanny sea-foam eyes. He looked like me, and like my father; as though the strange displacement that gave my uncle his somber weight cast a bright aura around his youngest child. In a crowded room with Rogan and me, you would always look at Rogan first.

"How was your day?" asked Aunt Pat.

"It was fine." My uncle bent to kiss the top of her head, then set a big hand on my shoulder. "Hi, Maddy. You setting a good example for these reprobates?"

"Trying to." I smiled weakly.

"Michael, you take care of those gutters like I asked you?"

Michael nodded, staring at his plate. "Yup."

"Good." My uncle's gaze barely touched the other boys as he turned to go upstairs to change. "I'll be down in a minute. Make me a drink, will you, Pat?" When he could be heard in the hall above us, everyone began to eat again.

I left soon after, not waiting for Uncle Richard to return, or for dessert. When I looked at Rogan across the table, I felt as though I must give off sparks.

And as I stood to go, I saw Michael staring at me.

"Make sure she rubs off on you," he called as Rogan walked me to the porch.

"Fuck you," said Rogan under his breath. Once we were outside, he bumped his forehead against mine. "Hey, I'll see you tomorrow, okay?"

"Okay," I said. "That was amazing. Up there . . ."

I tilted my head toward the upper stories.

Rogan grinned. "It was incredible." He looked the way he did on Christmas morning.

He went back inside, and I headed up the winding driveway. I'd gone about halfway when someone called out.

"Maddy!"

I turned. At the bottom of the hill, where the drive wound down to the carriage house, Aunt Kate stood and beckoned to me. "Come here!"

I lifted my hand in a wave and walked down to meet her, my shoulders hunched against the chill night wind. Aunt Kate looked beautiful and exotic as always, in green lizard-skin boots and a russet swing coat, her cheeks pink with cold and a paisley scarf loosely knotted around her neck. Someone was with her, a tall figure I didn't recognize; a man.

No surprise there. Aunt Kate had never married, but she had a lot of male friends. This caused great consternation among her family, especially the women, who took it as a personal affront that Kate had a (presumably) active sex life, as well as an intellectual one. None of her friends were stockbrokers or lawyers or doctors, which might have made their presence slightly more palatable, or at least comprehensible; and most of them appeared to fall under some vaguely defined rubric that identified them as artists of one sort or another: men who had too much hair or none at all, men who gave a blank look when someone brought up the Mets, but who had visited slightly louche destinations, Tangiers or Nepal or London or San Francisco. They had often read the same books as Rogan and me and, despite the disparity in our ages, sometimes listened to the same music.

This man, though, didn't look like the others. He was tall and thin, with a long, angular, ascetic face, and black hair cut very short. He wore a pinstriped suit, with a white shirt open at the neck. No tie. I slowed my steps.

But then Aunt Kate grasped the man's arm with one hand, her emerald ring glinting in the darkness; and with her other hand grabbed mine.

"So this is her?" The man looked at me and smiled. His dark eyes were kind, and amused. "The famous Madeline."

"Peter, I'd like you to meet my niece. Maddy, this is my friend Peter Sullivan. He's going to be teaching you."

"Uh, hi." We shook hands. I looked around, embarrassed and somewhat suspicious. A teacher?

"Next month I'll be teaching at St. Brendan's," explained Mr. Sullivan. "English. Taking over for Sister Alberta. You know she has breast cancer?"

I shook my head, as disconcerted by the realization that nuns could get cancer as that I had just heard a man utter the word *breast*.

"Oh, jeez. That's terrible," I said, then hastily added, "I mean that she's sick, not that you're a teacher."

"Madeline is *extremely talented*," said Aunt Kate. I blushed, though I was pleased. I was accustomed to hearing my parents say those words in the same tone they used to describe Ookie Connell— *He's a little slow.* "She and my nephew Rogan."

Mr. Sullivan cocked his head at Fairview. "Is he the one I hear singing?"

Aunt Kate nodded. "Yes, that's Rogan."

I stared at the ground, then glanced uneasily at Rogan's house.

Of course I knew people had heard Rogan sing. At night, he leaned out the window on purpose so his voice would carry. He'd sung at church.

Yet, somehow, I'd never thought that a *stranger* might hear him; someone who might, however remotely, matter in the world beyond Arden Terrace.

"He has an extraordinary voice," Mr. Sullivan went on. "Does he take lessons?"

"No, they won't train them," said Aunt Kate. She might have been referring to dogs that weren't housebroken.

Mr. Sullivan turned to me again. "What about you? Do you sing?"

He looked so open and encouraging that I felt a sudden desolation. As though everything good that had happened in my life was all a mistake—Rogan, outgrowing my glasses, being smart at schoolwork. Even the memory of what we'd seen earlier in the hidden attic; even the memory of Rogan himself, his taste, his hands, and his warmth and his soft skin . . . it all seemed distant and unreal. As though I'd opened a wonderful present, only to be told it was meant for one of my older, prettier sisters, and not for me.

"No," I said. "I can't sing."

Mr. Sullivan shrugged. "Hey, singing isn't everything." He smiled again.

Aunt Kate touched his arm. "You go on in. I need to talk with Maddy for a minute."

"Nice to meet you, Maddy," he said, and went into the carriage house.

"Come with me," my aunt said. "I left some things in the car."

I went with her into the garage beneath the carriage house, where her red Mustang was parked. She opened the back of the car, reached in, and handed me a bag from Gristede's, then gathered her purse and another grocery bag. "Just bring that up for me, thanks. Did you have dinner yet?"

"Yeah, with Rogan and everybody."

Aunt Kate wrinkled her nose. "Roast chicken?"

"It was good."

"It's the only thing they ever eat."

"They have turkey at Thanksgiving."

Aunt Kate sighed. "That's just a big chicken."

We walked out of the garage and climbed the rickety stairway up to the carriage house door. In the uppermost window shone the ghost light that my aunt kept burning, day or night. Above Fairview a full moon was just beginning to rise. Aunt Kate stopped, halfway up the steps, and looked at me.

"Listen, Maddy. I have something to tell you. I got tickets to take you and Rogan to see *Two Gentlemen of Verona*."

I looked at her blankly. "Who?"

"The play," she said. "By Shakespeare. A musical version; it's supposed to be very good."

"A play?"

"Yes. A play. On Broadway. It's at the St. James Theatre. Your birthdays are next week, I thought this would be fun."

I had never seen a play. Neither had Rogan. Nor, as far as I know, had any of our siblings or cousins. There had always been trips to the city, for baseball games and the circus and the Thanksgiving Day Parade, Christmas windows at Macy's, Radio City Music Hall and the Rockettes, Easter Mass at St. Patrick's Cathedral.

But a play?

"Really?" I said. "Me and Rogan?"

"Yes, really." She sounded angry. "And I haven't told your parents yet, so don't mention it until I've had the chance."

"I won't, I swear. Really?" I shook my head, then laughed. "I can't believe it."

"Neither can I."

She turned once more, her boots clattering up the stairs. At the top, she stopped again.

In the brilliant moonlight her face looked drawn, even gaunt. There were glints of silver at the roots of her sleek black hair. The beringed hands holding the Gristede's bag were crisscrossed with blue veins, and beneath the skin the bones of her fingers looked clawlike.

I had never before thought about how old she was, or even how she was related to me. She was a Tierney by birth. But she wasn't my father's sister, and she had never seemed old enough to be a great-aunt, like Aunt Margaret or Aunt Bella.

But now she looked old. Not ancient; just worn and tired. And resolute.

"Thank you, Maddy." She set her bag down outside the door, then reached for mine. "We have tickets for next Friday. I'll talk to everyone over the weekend."

"What if they say no?"

"I'll kidnap you." She smiled. "But they won't. Just don't make a big deal out of it, all right?"

"*They're* the ones who make a big deal out of it." I kicked at a step and looked back at Fairview. "Why? Why is it such a big goddamn deal? Why do they even care?"

Aunt Kate hesitated.

"They don't care," she finally said. "You know why? Because they have no talent. None of them—none of Madeline's children. Or, well, maybe they did, and she was just so vain and selfish she never encouraged any of them. She was insufferable. And once she stopped acting, all she cared about was money. After Rosco died, during the Depression—all she did was buy up real estate. Like it mattered—"

She gestured fiercely at Madeline's mansion. "As though any of this mattered. This—*stuff*. But that was all her children cared about. And when their children were born, your father and Richard and the rest, their parents never encouraged them, either. Rogan's father, Richard—he had a beautiful voice. Did you know that?"

I blinked in surprise. "No."

"Of course not." Aunt Kate laughed bitterly. "How would you? He never sang; it died on the vine. All those children, all those cousins— just like you and all your cousins, Maddy—and there was Richard with this voice. I used to listen to him—he'd sing when he was in the bathroom, it was the only place anyone was ever alone. 'Where or When . . .'"

She rubbed her eyes. "He never knew I was there. And after a little while I never heard him sing again."

"Did they—do something to him?"

"No, of course not." She shrugged dismissively. "But talent—if you don't encourage it, if you don't train it, it dies. It might run wild for a little while, but it will never mean anything. Like a wild horse. If you don't tame it and teach it to run on a track, to pace itself and bear a rider, it doesn't matter how fast it is. It's useless. And this family?"

She crossed her arms and stared at Fairview. "They have no use for 'useless.' If you can't make money, forget it."

"But actors make money. Madeline was famous. People on Broadway—they make money."

"That's not what your father or your uncle would call money, Maddy. Chump change. But it's not the money that matters. They lost faith. Madeline lost faith, and so the rest of them never had any."

She turned to gaze to where the woods crept up against the edge of the lawn—thin birches and sumac and a few old elm trees, all leafless now and black against the violet sky—then lifted her face toward the moon.

"You could say there were religious differences," she said.

The door opened, and Mr. Sullivan peered out. "Do you need help bringing things in?"

Aunt Kate shook her head. "Thank you, Peter, no. We were just saying good-bye."

She stepped inside with the groceries.

"I'll see you in a few weeks, Maddy," said Mr. Sullivan, and he closed the door.

I walked slowly back to my house. A light was on in Rogan's window, and I tried to hear his voice in my head, to will him to appear and sing.

But even in my imagination I couldn't give voice to anything that sounded like him. I reached the street and saw my own house, its windows bright and the television blaring from the living room, my mother calling upstairs to my sister. I pulled Rogan's jacket tight around me and went home.

❖ ❖ ❖

ROGAN CALLED ME EARLY THE NEXT MORNING.

"I'm not gonna be around this weekend." He sounded bereft. "I have to go with my parents to see John at Holy Cross. We won't be back till tomorrow night."

"Oh, God." I stretched the phone cord as far as it would go and looked out the front window, down to his house. "Are you downstairs?"

"Yeah." There was a fitful motion in a dark window. "Can you see me?"

"Yeah." I told him about going to the theater with Aunt Kate. "You think they'll say yes?"

"Yours probably will."

This was true. My parents' attitude in most things was one of benign neglect. Or perhaps it was just fatigue, spiking into occasional rages of guilt-fueled retribution for minor infractions, a bad grade, or the expression of an imprudent political view.

"Well, maybe she'll tell them first. That'd make it easier for you."

"Maybe." He sounded grim. "I gotta go. I'll call you when I get back."

I spent the day in a funk. The weather was glorious; my friend Nancy called to see if I wanted to go shopping but I said no. All I could think of was Rogan, all I *wanted* to think of was Rogan, and what we'd seen in the secret attic above Fairview. I paced the house, restless and angry, avoiding my mother (who would have put me to work) and picking fights with my sisters, until late afternoon when my father returned home from playing golf.

"I'm going to five o'clock Mass." He announced this every Saturday as though it were news. "Anyone want to come?"

"I will."

My father looked at me with mild surprise. Since Rogan had stopped singing in church, I attended the sloths' Mass at noon on Sunday. "Well, get ready," he said.

An idea had come to me. I sat in church and worked out the details, then rode home with my father.

"Rogan went with Uncle Richard and Aunt Pat to see John at college," I said.

My father looked absently out the car window. "Yes, I know."

I made my voice sound as casual as possible. "Do you know if Michael and Thomas went?"

"No, I don't, dear." My father frowned. "Well, yes, they might have. I think they did; I think Pat said they were going to stay with the Garlands."

I nodded, holding my breath in case he wondered why I'd asked. But he said nothing more.

Early Sunday morning my father went to play golf again. I slouched around the house till my mother and sisters left for church. Then I pulled on Rogan's jacket and hurried across the street to Fairview. I walked as quickly as I could down the drive, hoping I wouldn't run into my aunt. Not that she would have questioned why I was there, or cared.

But I didn't want to see anyone. I darted onto the porch, pulled open the great oaken front door, and slipped into the foyer, closing the door carefully behind me.

It was the first time I'd ever been in Fairview when no one was home. The rugs and old furniture made it look more like a shabby museum than a house where people lived. Golden sun streamed through the downstairs windows, but did nothing to warm the place. It was spooky and silent and cold. I felt uneasy, even frightened, with none of the exhilaration I felt when Rogan and I did something forbidden. I stood at the foot of the broad curved staircase, shivering, and watched my breath cloud the air.

"Hello?" I called out softly. No one was there.

I went upstairs. When I reached the third floor my anxiety faded somewhat, though as I walked into Rogan's room, I didn't feel the relief I'd expected. Without him, the old nursery looked impossibly, almost cruelly barren and sad. It was even colder than downstairs. There was a glass of water next to the unmade bed, a flashlight, a notebook I prodded with my foot. Rogan's school clothes were strewn across the floor, corduroy trousers and a new jacket, dirty socks and T-shirts.

I picked up a flannel shirt and brought it to my face. It smelled of Rogan, smoky, slightly acrid. It smelled warm. I removed my jacket and my own shirt, and pulled on his. I closed the door to his room, got the flashlight and turned it on, and went into the outer attic.

I stepped gingerly between cardboard boxes until I reached the back wall. I balanced the flashlight as best I could, then began to pull out the stack of cartons. Once or twice it nearly toppled onto me, and I swore under my breath until I could get everything back into place. Finally I moved the cartons enough that I could unlatch the hidden door and open it enough for me to slip inside. I pulled the door closed behind me and shone the flashlight across the narrow space.

Everything was as we'd left it, blankets in disarray and the few books scattered. The loose board hadn't budged. I leaned the flashlight against the door, knelt, and folded the blankets and stacked the books; retrieved the flashlight and turned it off, and sat cross-legged in the darkness.

Silence. I held my breath as long as I could, and listened. But there was still nothing.

"Rogan," I whispered.

I lay down on the blankets, pulled up the flannel shirt until it covered my face. I breathed in his scent, squeezed my eyes tightly shut even though there was nothing to see. I found the place where the blankets still smelled of us, murmured his name, and tried to bring back the sound of Rogan singing, his voice strung between us like the glimmering thread that stretched from Arden Terrace to the city. Only the faintest echo of it came to me; but when it did, there was an instant when I imagined I saw Rogan moving beneath me, darker even than the room, darker than anything; the shadow of the song.

I shuddered and lay without moving, my tear-streaked face pressed against his shirt. Minutes passed. I listened to my heartbeat slow. Then I heard another sound.

It was the same rhythmic tapping I'd heard the other day with Rogan, the same oddly surging whistle, like wind or waves. I pulled my shirt down, wriggled forward until I could touch the wall. I pried my fingers under the board until it came loose, set it down, and looked through the opening.

At first I thought my vision was blurred. The toy theater was exactly where I'd last seen it—perhaps four inches from the wall, lit by those same unearthly footlights.

But now the stage seemed distorted and unsteady, as if it were underwater. I rubbed my eyes, squinting to get a better view, then sucked my breath in.

Snow was falling. Not everywhere. Only behind the proscenium, on the tiny stage itself.

Not real snow. Fake snow.

And not white but silver and palest blue, finer than any glitter I had ever seen, finer than salt or powder, like something that would flake from the most microscopic shining matter you could imagine: glitter's glitter. It sifted onto the stage floor and whirled in tiny eddies, as though stirred by tiny unseen feet, and where it fell too near the footlights there were infinitesimal flares of gold and scarlet, and the most delicate fragrance, roses mingled with scorched sugar.

I stared at it entranced, barely registering the shift in light toward the back of the stage where the topiary trees, now crystalline and opal-colored, gave way to knife-edged mountains and a snow-covered beach beneath a night sky, with a full moon snared in the rigging of a spectral shipwreck and a fluttering shadow like a moth's moving slowly, as though injured, across the white dunes. All the while the tapping continued, and that soft insistent whistle, like a steady indrawn breath.

Without thinking, I lifted my hand and extended it through the gap in the wall. I stretched it toward the stage just beyond the apron, until my fingers gleamed silver-blue in the footlights. I felt no cold, no heat. Just a faint tingling like a mild electrical shock, as though hair-sized needles stabbed my fingertips. I waited to see if anything changed, if something noticed my intrusion.

Nothing did. The fake snow fell and drifted and whirled. The weird noises didn't stop.

Finally I withdrew my hand. It was unmarked, and felt no different when I rubbed it against my cheek.

But suddenly I felt scared—that I *didn't* feel anything. That something so strange and inexplicable could leave no lasting mark, no trace that I had encountered it at all: not a scratch, not a shift in body temperature, nothing but a fleeting memory of sound and light and motion.

I shoved the board back into place, then scrambled in the dark for the flashlight. I stumbled back into the outer attic, knocked over a carton, and sat, heart hammering, as I listened for a shout of discovery from below.

But the house remained empty. I lurched from the attic into Rogan's room and blinked, shocked to see that it was still daylight.

The alarm clock read 1:05. I tore off his flannel shirt and flung it onto the floor, pulled my own shirt back on, and grabbed my jacket and fled downstairs. I ran into no one in the house, no one outside, and no one when I got back to my house.

❖ ❖ ❖

"YOUR AUNT KATE WANTS TO TAKE YOU TO SEE A show," my mother announced at dinner that night.

I feigned surprise. "A show?"

She nodded. "A Broadway show. Something by Shakespeare. *The Merchant of Venice*, I think."

I caught myself before I corrected her. "Can I go?"

"I don't see why not. It's for your birthday. And it's Friday, so it's not a school night. She wanted to take Rogan, too, I think. Hal? Is it all right with you?"

She looked at my father. He swallowed his mouthful of baked potato, then said, "Yes, Kate mentioned it. She said she'd take you to dinner at Rosoff's beforehand."

I said, "That'll be fun."

"Make sure you wear something nice," said my mother.

I didn't get a chance to talk to Rogan until the following afternoon. It was our fifteenth birthday, but we'd already decided not to
make a big deal out of it. Nobody else was, except for Aunt Kate. He
was waiting for me in the school parking yard.

"Wait'll you see what I got," he said as we walked down the hill
toward Arden Terrace. "Un-fucking-believable. In-fucking-credible."

"What?"

"John gave me his old sound system. He has a new roommate
this year, this guy Jeff. He's got an amazing stereo so John said I could
have his."

"For your birthday?"

"Nah, he didn't even remember that till I told him. But isn't that
cool?"

I smiled. "It's great."

"And dig this—this guy Jeff, he gave me a bunch of albums. I
listened to some last night. It's wild stuff, Maddy."

He swayed back and forth, singing snatches of a song I didn't
recognize. He laughed. "Man, I am *so* psyched."

We reached the bottom of the hill and turned down the road that
led to Arden Terrace. Acorns rolled underfoot, hidden by the yellow
leaves banked against the curb. Rogan grabbed a handful and tossed
them across the road.

"Did Aunt Kate talk to your parents?" I said.

"Not yet."

"Maybe she did today."

"Maybe," he said, unconcerned.

We reached Fairview. I still hadn't told him about sneaking

into the attic the day before. Upstairs, Rogan kicked at the door to Michael's room, to make sure no one was inside.

"Come here," said Rogan, and pulled me to him. We kissed in the hallway, then went into Rogan's room and closed the door. "Check this out, Maddy."

The turntable sat on the floor by the wall. Rogan began sorting through a small pile of records beside it.

"Here," he said.

He put the record on the turntable and handed me the sleeve. It showed a cartoon of a subway entrance, with pink smoke welling up from the black tunnel.

"What—"

Rogan put his hand over my mouth. "Shhh. Listen."

He played me two songs about a girl named Jane.

"That's us, Maddy," he said when the songs were over. "Our lives were saved by rock and roll."

I gave him a funny look. "That's more like your life. I can't sing."

"It's both of us." He grabbed my arm and dragged me toward the attic door. "Come on, Mad-girl—"

Afterward we lay side by side in the dark. Rogan pried the board loose and we gazed at the glimmering stage, our own tiny cosmos. There was no snow this time. Wherever the stage was, whatever it was supposed to represent, it seemed to be the middle of the night. The footlights cast a flickering cobalt glow across the stage.

I told Rogan what I had seen the day before. Snow; a full moon.

"Do you think there's anyone there?" he wondered, and stroked my back. "That we can't see?"

"I don't know."

I touched my fingers to his lips, then kissed him. I was afraid to guess at what might be there, beyond the tiny stage; afraid to give a name to what we saw there, just as I couldn't give a name to what I felt for my cousin.

Magic; love.

Endless longing; a face you'd known since childhood, since birth almost; a body that moved as though it were your own. These were things you never spoke of, things you never hoped for; things you could never admit to. Things you'd die for, and die of.

"Rogan," I whispered.

"What?" He turned to me, and his eyes gleamed peacock-blue in the footlights. "Maddy? Why are you crying?"

"Nothing. Rogan." He put his arms around me and I trembled. "Just you."

❖ ❖ ❖

ROGAN'S PARENTS DIDN'T MAKE A BIG DEAL OVER him going to the play.

"They didn't care," he said a few days later. "They're going out Friday anyway. All they said was don't get lost in the city."

"Maybe because it's Aunt Kate? Or Shakespeare."

"Yeah, maybe." He sounded unconvinced.

After school on Friday we changed for the theater. I wore a long granny skirt and embroidered blouse and a macramé vest, and my new Frye boots. Rogan put on a clean flannel shirt and a different corduroy jacket than the one he'd worn to school that day.

We walked together from Fairview down the drive to Aunt Kate's house. It felt different: the two of us together in the waning daylight, wearing what passed for nice clothes, with a common destination and our parents' approval. Inside the carriage house, Aunt Kate hurried about, looking for her purse, the tickets, her expensive lipstick. She looked elegant—glamorous—in black velvet cigarette pants and a cream-colored silk blouse, a cropped bolero jacket. She wore no jewelry other than her emerald ring. Suddenly she stopped and stared at me.

"Maddy." Her eyes narrowed. "Don't you have a coat?"

I shrugged. "Just that yellow one. It didn't really go."

Aunt Kate winced. "That thing from Sears? You're right. That's an awful coat."

She stood, thinking; then turned and ran upstairs. Minutes later she returned, holding what looked like a blanket.

"Here." She opened the door, walked out onto the top of the stairs, and shook the blanket vigorously. "This has been in storage all these years, I just had it dry-cleaned this summer. See if it fits."

She stepped back inside and handed it to me. Not a blanket but a long cape, of royal-blue velvet lined with white satin, with three gold buttons at the top to fasten it.

"That was your great-grandmother's opera cape," Aunt Kate said as I pulled it on. "Madeline used to wear it after every performance. Wait—"

She adjusted it over my shoulders, then buttoned it. "Those are real gold. Wow. Maddy! It fits. It looks *great*. Utterly glamorous. Go look at yourself," she urged.

I walked into the living room and stood before the big old mirror there. Someone else stared back, me but not me. The deep-blue velvet made my hair look glossy chestnut, not mousy. My eyes seemed to have darkened as well, to midnight blue or indigo. I put my arm out and whirled, the folds rippling around me like waves.

"Holy Batcape, Batman," said Rogan.

I turned to him. "What do you think? Am I glamorous?"

"It looks fantastic. Can I try it on?"

"No," said Aunt Kate. "We need to go, the train's in twenty minutes. Come on—"

Rosoff's, the restaurant where we ate, was warm and wood paneled, crowded with theatergoers and filled with Broadway memorabilia—ancient photographs, old etchings, framed faded *Playbills*.

"It's like eating in my house," said Rogan. I couldn't tell if this was a complaint or not. "Better food, though."

He'd ordered the chicken.

After dinner we walked to the St. James Theatre. Our seats were Orchestra, Row E, Center.

"This is where the drama critics always sit," Aunt Kate explained. "Best seats in the house. You're close enough to see the actors sweat and spit when they talk."

Rogan laughed. "Hey, *that's* glamorous."

"It's work, Rogan." Aunt Kate delicately balanced her *Playbill* on a velvet-clad knee. "If the actors are good enough, you don't mind seeing their sweat."

"What about their spit?" asked Rogan. "Do I have to like their spit, too?"

Aunt Kate frowned and began to read her program. Rogan and I did the same.

"Hey." He jabbed a finger at the cast list. "The guy who wrote this is the same guy who wrote *Hair*! Maybe they'll take their clothes off."

We looked at Aunt Kate with renewed admiration.

The play was perfect. How could it have been otherwise? It was the first one either of us had ever seen, barring school productions at Christmas and St. Patrick's Day. The script was bowdlerized Shakespeare, the music cheerful and relentlessly contemporary. There were black people in the cast, and Puerto Ricans—an astonishing revelation—also sexual innuendos that seemed to be inherent to the original play.

Our admiration for Aunt Kate, and Shakespeare, became immeasurable.

After the play, we spilled onto the street with throngs of happily chattering people. I felt not just exhilarated but exalted, the way I did when Rogan sang. He sang now, a tune from the show he'd already memorized, walking along Broadway and turning on his heels, his voice rising above the crowd in a charmed, eerie falsetto. People looked at him in wonder and delight, his beautiful face and long hair, eyes closed as he walked backward, certain somehow that he wouldn't fall.

We talked about the play the whole way back on the train, then in Aunt Kate's car.

"I don't want it to stop," said Rogan as we walked out of the garage beneath her carriage house. He didn't sound disappointed, but anguished. "Why does it have to end?"

Aunt Kate dropped her keys into her purse. "Well, it doesn't. I got tickets next week for *Butley*."

Rogan and I looked at each other, then burst out laughing.

"Thank you!"

"Jesus, Aunt Kate, really?"

"Shhh!" She cut us off sternly. "Hush. I haven't spoken to them yet. But yes. Good night, Rogan."

She kissed him, then beckoned at me. "Come upstairs, Maddy. That cape stays here."

I waved good-bye at Rogan. His voice echoed through the chill air until he entered Fairview, and the autumn night grew silent.

Inside I took off the cape and gave it back to my aunt, who folded it carefully then went upstairs. I stood in the living room, alone, and looked at the framed photographs of my great-great-grandmother on the wall. Madeline as Rosalind, her hair cropped short so she resembled a sly boy; Madeline as Gwendolen in *The Importance of Being Earnest*, a wicked glint in her eye as she pretended to read her diary. Madeline as Anya in *The Cherry Orchard*; as Mrs. Pinchwife, Cordelia, and Cleopatra, and the title character in *Major Barbara*.

She looked different in each picture. Recognizably herself yet somehow, remarkably, older or younger or cunning or heartbroken by turns. Her adult career had been prolific but short-lived. The pictures displayed an eternal ingenue, an eternal boy-girl: Rosalind and Viola but never Hedda Gabler; never Lady Macbeth. There were no photographs of her as an old woman.

I turned and slowly walked over to the mirror. Whatever enchantment I had felt or carried earlier when I'd worn the cape and sat inside
the theater was gone now. I looked like an ordinary fifteen-year-old
girl wearing new boots that were already scuffed, and clothes from
Sears and Gimbels.

"Okay, that's squared away," called Aunt Kate. "We can get it out
again next weekend."

I looked over to see my aunt coming down the stairs.

"I'm not glamorous," I said. I didn't feel sad, just resigned. "Rogan
is more glamorous than I am. Everyone is."

My aunt walked over to stand beside me at the mirror. She pulled
a stray wisp of hair behind my ear and stared at our reflections.

"Rogan's not glamorous."

"How can you even say that?" I looked away so she wouldn't see
tears in my eyes. "He's so beautiful. And what you said about talent—
he has that *voice . . .*"

"No, Maddy. Beauty isn't glamour. It's not the same thing at all."
She stroked my hair. "Do you know what *glamour* means?"

"Beautiful." I spat the word. "Perfect, talented—"

"That's not what it means, Madeline." She shook her head.
"*Glamour*—it has the same root as the word *grammar*. It is a kind
of knowledge, of learning. That means it's something that can be
taught. It can be learned."

She put her hands on my shoulders and straightened them. "Your
great-great-grandmother wasn't beautiful, Maddy."

"Gee, thanks. Since I'm supposed to *look* like her."

"You're actually much prettier than she was," said Aunt Kate. "You have beautiful eyes, your skin's cleared up. And you're taller. She was quite petite; these days you need to be tall. And your teeth are much better—she never had her teeth fixed."

"That's not grammar," I said sullenly. "None of that is stuff I learned."

"No. But you can learn other things. Words, how to speak and walk. How to make your voice carry. Diction."

"That sounds horrible."

"Think of it like this: you're building a house, a beautiful house, a little bit at a time out of all these things—your voice, your body, your memory, how you move. If you do it right, if you put all the elements together, something happens. Something comes to live in that space you've made, inside you. Then you go onstage and people see it. They see you, but they also see this other—thing—that you've created. That you've built, that you're inside of."

"Oh, right," I said. "Like now I'm a goddamn carpenter."

She laughed. "It's like Latin, Maddy. That's grammar, too. But you studied it and learned it and now you're good at it. Your mind is attuned to it. *You* have a *gift*." She turned me so that I looked at her squarely. "You have talent."

"Not like Rogan."

"Rogan is talented, yes." She sounded impatient. "But the tail wags the dog with him."

"I don't even know what means."

She sighed. "It's late. You'd better get home; we need to stay in everyone's good graces."

I walked to the door, contrite. "Thanks, Aunt Kate. It was great—it was the best time I ever had."

"It's only going to get better," she said, and kissed me good night.

At home I went into the living room and found the enormous old dictionary that had been my grandfather's. I opened it to *glamour* and read a definition similar to what Aunt Kate had told me; but also something else.

A corruption of GRAMMAR, meaning GRAMARYE.
1. An enchantment or spell; an illusion of beauty.

I set the book down and looked out the window. In Aunt Kate's carriage house a single lamp burned, and in Rogan's window as well. Ghost lights; gramarye.

I turned the light off in the living room and went upstairs to bed.

❖ ❖ ❖

WE DIDN'T JUST SEE *BUTLEY.* OVER THE NEXT FEW weeks, Rogan and I saw *Pippin* and *Measure for Measure* and *A Streetcar Named Desire* and *Jumpers* and *A Little Night Music.* We went on Friday nights, and sometimes Saturday, and even weekend matinees. A few times Mr. Sullivan accompanied us, along with Aunt Kate.

This was embarrassing at first, and neither Rogan nor I ever mentioned it to our parents. We still couldn't figure out what had happened—did Aunt Kate lie to them? Had they undergone some weird middle-aged conversion? Had they all gone senile?

But, no, Aunt Kate made no secret of what we were doing.

She asked for permission each time, always announcing we'd go to Rosoff's first for dinner, or for lunch if it was a matinee. Our parents remained as intransigent as ever otherwise; Rogan's even more so, as his grades, never good, had gotten worse. He'd snuck off twice to hang out with the band fronted by his brother's friend Derek, something I got furious about when he told me.

"They'll kill you if they find out." We were in the secret attic, naked. Rogan had gotten some condoms from Derek, which was how I came to learn about the band rehearsals. "That is so stupid, Rogan."

"Don't you start." He drew away from me. "Stupid. I know, I'm a fucking retard."

"Shut up." I pulled him back toward me and kissed him. His mouth was liquid, his breath pungent with hashish: another gift from Derek. "Don't ever say that. You're brilliant."

It had become more difficult for us to get time together alone—we were with Aunt Kate most of our free time. And my parents made it clear that they didn't want me constantly at Fairview.

"I want you to spend time with your friends," my mother said.

"Rogan's my friend."

My mother gave me a keen look. "He's your cousin, Maddy." I knew it was a warning.

Now, in the attic, I rolled on top of him. My head bumped the ceiling, and plaster fragments rained onto us.

"Be careful," murmured Rogan. "Let's look . . ."

He gently tugged the board loose so we could peer inside the wall. It never changed—or no, the stage changed every time we looked at it, the footlights glimmering green or cobalt or vermilion, the backdrops shifting as well to signal dawn, or late afternoon, midsummer or deepest winter. Sometimes it snowed; sometimes by some trick of the light the stage seemed slashed with rain or sleet. Once we heard odd chirping strings, like a cricket orchestra, and once a crackling that I realized must be the rattle of a tiny thunder sheet.

But the toy theater itself never changed. The proscenium with its paired masks and delicate frieze of languid Muses; the gauzy red curtains, bound in place with gilt thread—day to day, week to week, all remained unaltered. The invisible audience rustled and sighed, the invisible actors moved, if they moved at all, in steps unknown to my cousin and me.

It was late October. One Monday we arrived at school to find that Mr. Sullivan was now an English teacher. Sister Alberta had gone into St. Joseph's Hospital for treatment.

"Will she be back?" a girl asked.

Mr. Sullivan smiled wistfully. "I don't know. I hope so."

"I don't," said another girl, and everyone laughed.

Immediately, Mr. Sullivan became an object of much speculation. He was handsome, though maybe not as good-looking as Mr. Becker, who also taught English, and who was rumored to smoke pot.

But Mr. Sullivan was mysterious. He had been in the seminary— why hadn't Rogan and I known that?—and he'd also been an actor, with a small recurring part as Dr. Burke on *One Life to Live*. He'd been in a commercial for Irish Spring soap, a commercial that still aired and which I'd seen at least a dozen times.

"Why didn't you tell us?" demanded Rogan after class one day, when Mr. Sullivan admitted that, yes, that was him in the commercial, him in the boat, wearing a tweed walking cap and speaking with a brogue so patently false I was ashamed for him.

"You didn't ask," said Mr. Sullivan mildly. "And I can't play favorites in school."

We'd noted that already, when we tried in vain to get him to change the curriculum for Freshman English.

"These books," said Rogan. He began to tick them off on his fingers. "*Billy Budd. The Catcher in the Rye. A Separate Peace. Romeo and Juliet. Lord of the Flies.* Every single ninth-grade book, everyone dies! It's depressing."

Mr. Sullivan tipped his head. "Good point. But you still have to read them."

"Why?" Rogan stared at him challengingly, almost belligerently. "Can you give me one good goddamn reason why?"

"Enough," snapped Mr. Sullivan. "Everyone, get out your copies of *The Diary of Anne Frank.*"

Rogan's defiance bled into our trips to the city as well. We were with Aunt Kate on the train back home after seeing *The Country Wife.* Aunt Kate was seated, reading *The New Yorker.* Rogan and I were goofing around, swinging on the poles by the train doors. As the train approached the 125th Street Station, a small group of people gathered around us, waiting to get out.

The train stopped. The little crowd stepped out onto the platform. So did Rogan.

I gaped in disbelief. He took a step backward, grinning broadly, and as the doors closed gave me a little wave and mouthed *Bye-bye.*

"Holy shit," I said.

The train pulled out of the station. Aunt Kate looked up, eye-brows raised. "What?"

"Rogan." I pointed uselessly at the platform disappearing behind us. "He—"

I collapsed, laughing hysterically, onto the floor of the train.

Aunt Kate was not amused. "That brainless idiot," she fumed, nostrils white with rage. "Getting off in *Harlem* in the *middle of the night*?"

"It's only eleven," I protested. She looked daggers at me.

"Don't you say a word. Did you put him up to it?"

"No!"

At the next stop she dragged me from the train onto the platform. We waited, hardly speaking, for the next southbound train. It was a short distance between Melrose and 125th Street, but there were few trains that late at night. I began to grow anxious.

"Should we call the police?" I asked.

"And say what? That there's a white boy wandering around Har-lem?"

By the time we got a train and it stopped at 125th Street, nearly an hour had passed. Aunt Kate grabbed me again and yanked me onto the platform.

There, sitting sheepishly on a bench, was Rogan. Beside him sat a tall black woman, dressed as elegantly as my aunt, her hands crossed resolutely on one knee as she stared straight ahead. I couldn't tell if she was a young woman whose hair had turned prematurely white, or an old woman who had drunk from the same Fountain of Youth as Aunt Kate.

As my aunt approached her, the woman stood. "I take it this is your young man?" Aunt Kate nodded. "I found him roaming the street like a chicken with its head cut off."

The woman gave Rogan a severe look, then lightly cuffed his long red hair. "Better for him if that *was* cut off. He said he was interested in the night life."

She and Aunt Kate regarded each other measuringly. I felt the same jaw-dropping disbelief as when Rogan had stepped from the carriage: this woman and my aunt *knew each other.*

But then a voice boomed across the platform, announcing the arrival of the next northbound train.

"Thank you very much," said Aunt Kate. She nodded respectfully.

"I'm just glad I happened by," the woman said. She waited until the train stopped at the platform, smiled, and left.

Aunt Kate pointed at Rogan. "You. Stand up and get on that train. No more nonsense."

"Did you see anything?" I whispered to Rogan as the train pulled away.

"Not really. A little." He turned to stare longingly at the streets below us, desolate and windswept, a few solitary figures hurrying along the sidewalk. "It was cool. Next time I'm staying."

The announcement for the school play went up the following Monday. Rogan and I were walking down the hall, when we saw a few people gathered in front of the bulletin board outside the English Department.

"Bad news, bro," someone said to Rogan. "It's not a musical."

I glanced at Rogan. His jaw tightened, his face froze into a mask of resignation and suppressed anger so intense that, without thinking, I touched his arm. He shrugged me off and pushed through the group to look at the audition sheet.

St. Brendan's Sock & Buskin Club

Annual Play Tryouts for

TWELFTH NIGHT, or What You Will

by William Shakespeare

Friday, November 12, 3:00

See Mr. Sullivan for details

"*Twelfth Night*." I felt a swell of excitement, despite Rogan's disappointment. "That's the one about the twins."

"Shakespeare," said Rogan in disgust. "Who the hell does Shakespeare in high school?"

"But you *like* Shakespeare." I looked at him as though he'd forgotten my name. "That's why you stole my book!"

"*Romeo and Juliet*. I fucking hate that play."

"This isn't *Romeo and Juliet*. This is the one with the twins—"

"They all have twins," said Rogan. But he sounded less dismissive. "*Twelfth Night* is the shipwreck, right?"

I nodded, and his expression softened. He glanced around to make sure no one saw, then touched my hand. "Yeah, I remember. I always liked that one."

"Twins." My excitement deepened. "Rogan, we could be the main parts! Because we really could *be* twins, they wouldn't have to make us up, we already look alike—"

"Yeah, yeah, you're right." He nodded thoughtfully. "That could be cool. You'd have to get your hair cut. And do something about the color . . ."

The bell rang. The corridor filled with students rushing to class.

"We should practice," I said. "For the audition. I'll find a copy at my house or your place. There has to be one somewhere."

"Yeah, well, good luck finding anything in that shithole," he said. "I gotta go."

That afternoon I ransacked my house for a copy of the play. We only knew the story from Madeline's old edition of *Tales from Shakespeare*, with Arthur Rackham's pretty, fairy-tale evocations of winsome lovers and thwarted rulers.

The copy I eventually found seemed a relic from another world entirely: a once-sturdy, extremely ugly high school edition that had once belonged to my father, with cursory annotations to the text explaining the action though not the more unsavory jokes. The book had a pukey green cover and no illustrations, save a black-and-white frontispiece of a mincing, Mephistophelean figure in a stiff ruff and pointy shoes. Malvolio, I guessed, the vain Puritanical steward who becomes the victim of a cruel practical joke. Someone—my father?—had defaced the picture, adding glasses, a Hitler mustache, and buckteeth.

But the text seemed complete, as far as I could tell. At least there was no mention of it having been abridged or modified for a young audience. I skipped through the opening pages to Viola's first lines.

Act 1, Scene 2

Enter Viola, a Captain, and Sailors

Viola: *What country, friends, is this?*
Captain: *This is Illyria, lady.*
Viola: *And what should I do in Illyria?*
My brother, he is in Elysium.

"'My brother, he is in Elysium . . .'"

I read the lines aloud; then went back to the beginning and read it all through, straight to the end. When I was finished, I went across the street to Fairview. Michael was downstairs, his lanky form folded into an armchair, eating a bowl of cereal and watching TV.

"Hey, Maddy," he said without glancing at me. "If you're looking for Rogan, he's not here. He went over to Derek's to practice."

"He did?"

Something in my tone made him look up. "He'll be back. Pretty soon, probably. Derek said he had to do something at five. You want me to tell him you came by?"

"No. I guess I'll just wait. If you think he'll be here." I held up the book. "We were going to practice for the play tryouts. The auditions are Friday."

Michael dug into his Cap'n Crunch. "Oh, yeah. I heard everyone's bummed it's not a musical. That new guy, Sullivan. Breaking with tradition. I didn't think Rogan was going to try out; I felt kinda bad for him. Since they weren't doing a musical. I know he really wanted to sing. He would've gotten the lead, too, whatever they did. He's got such a fucking amazing voice."

A sort of darkness swept over me. I felt cold and dizzy, as though I'd arrived someplace for a big party, only to find I'd gotten the date wrong and missed it, everything had happened weeks before, and I'd never even known.

"You want something to eat?" Michael held out the box of Cap'n Crunch. "You look kinda weird."

"I'm okay."

Rogan arrived half an hour later. He looked happy and wind-blown, sweeping into the house in a flurry of dead leaves.

"Hey, Mad-girl." He grinned when he saw me. I could smell smoke on him, cigarettes and marijuana. The uncanny blue-green eyes were bloodshot. "Whatcha doing?'

I gave him a wan smile and held up the book. "I thought maybe we could rehearse?"

"Oh, yeah. Right. I meant to tell you, the guys wanted to practice, we're doing some new stuff. But we can do it now if you want. That okay?"

He tipped his head to make sure Michael wasn't paying attention, then rubbed my arm. "Come on, let's go to my room."

Upstairs we read the entire play. Rogan took all the male parts. I took the female ones, and gave perfunctory readings to everyone save Viola. I was surprised at how easily Rogan handled all the lines, not just Sebastian's.

"I thought you hated Shakespeare," I said.

"Just *Romeo and Juliet*. This one's pretty funny."

We stopped often, to peruse the facile annotations and try to imagine what the stage directions would be.

"This is, like, a dirty joke." Rogan tapped the page where Malvolio read aloud from a forged love letter, supposedly penned by his employer, Olivia. "*'These be her very c's, her u's, and her t's, and thus makes she her great P's.'* He's talking about a cunt."

I whacked him with the book.

"Hey, I didn't say it! Shakespeare did."

We reached the end. For a minute, neither of us spoke.

"The girl has the bigger part," Rogan said at last. He didn't look at me. "Viola. The play's really about her. Not Sebastian. The boy twin's hardly onstage at all."

"He's on at the end," I said quickly. "He has that great swordfight where Sebastian wins, where he duels Andrew Aguecheek. All his scenes are just toward the end of the play, that's all."

"I guess," said Rogan.

But we both knew he was right. It was Viola's show, at least the way the words read on the page.

"Come on," I said. "It'd be so great, Rogan, we'd be up there together, it would be like—"

I wanted to say, *It would be like when we're alone.* Like when Rogan murmured, *You can't breathe,* and I couldn't breathe, because desire and arousal choked me, because I breathed nothing but him; he was my air, my element; everything.

But being onstage together wouldn't be like that. How could it? Nothing would ever be like that.

The bleak horror I'd felt earlier returned; the sense that I had somehow missed the real meaning of the world, which everyone but me had always known.

"It would be okay, I guess." Rogan shrugged. He ran his hand along the back of my neck and gave me a sweet, stoned smile. "Hey, don't look like that! I'll do it—we'll do it. You're right, it'll be fun . . ."

He leaned down to kiss me. I shut my eyes and imagined us in the close darkness of the attic, the toy theater tossing its phantom starlight on our bodies as we moved together, like some strange articulated toy.

"What's going on?"

We sat up so violently our jaws cracked. The copy of *Twelfth Night* spun across the floor, to where Rogan's mother stood in the doorway. She stared at us, mouth pursed between uncertainty and angry disapproval.

"Why is this door closed?" she demanded.

"We're rehearsing." I scrambled to pick up the book and showed it to her. "This play by Shakespeare, the auditions are Friday. We're going to try out for it."

Aunt Pat barely glanced at the book.

"Leave this door open," she said. "Rogan, you need to get ready for dinner."

She stood and waited for me to leave.

"I'll see you tomorrow," I said to Rogan, without meeting his eyes.

"Yeah, see you."

At the bottom of the steps, Aunt Pat stopped. She gave me an icy look.

"You need to find other things to do with yourself, Madeline. You're too old for this. You're both too old for this."

She stared at me until I left.

At dinner I showed the battered copy of *Twelfth Night* to my parents and my sister.

"Do you remember doing that?" I pointed to poor Malvolio's scribbled face.

My father took the book and frowned, riffled the pages, then gave it back to me.

"I'm afraid I don't remember it, dear," he said, in the tone he might use if a small child attempted and failed to tell a joke.

"It's got your name in it."

"Mmm."

While we ate dessert I asked, "Is it okay if I dye my hair?"

"No," said my mother. "Are you out of your mind?"

"Nice try." My sister smirked.

I glared at her and went on. "It's for the play at school. The main parts are twins. Rogan and I are trying out together. If we get it I'll need to look like him."

"Then make him get his hair cut," said my father tersely.

"I won't even do it unless I get the part," I pleaded.

"No," my mother repeated. "Don't ask again."

The auditions were held right after school on Friday. Rogan and I made a few halfhearted attempts to practice lines during the week.

But there was only one afternoon when we had several hours to ourselves, and we spent those hours in the attic.

"That's really stupid," I said when we first crawled in and Rogan lit a cigarette. "Someone could smell it."

"My parents smoke. And no one's home now."

I looked at the overflowing ashtray. "It could start a fire."

Rogan stubbed it out and pulled me to him. "I don't need a ciga-rette to do that. Come on, they'll be home soon—"

Fear of discovery made the time feel urgent, almost frantic. Even the toy theater seemed irradiated by our anxiety. Its footlights dimmed to a glowering dull red, and indistinct shadows cloaked the topiary trees and faraway shipwreck, as though they had been curso-rily sketched onto the backdrop. Rogan lay beside me, his face sus-pended above mine; but I couldn't see him, only smell him, his breath resinous with marijuana, and hear the broken rhythm of his breath-ing: silence, then a sound like a sigh, then silence once more.

"Rogan." I pressed my hand to his face and he kissed my palm. "I can hardly see you."

"That's because I'm not really here," he said.

On Friday, I was surprised by how many people showed up for the auditions. There were students scattered all over the auditorium, the usual drama crowd but other people, too. A bunch of girls from different English classes, and quite a few upper-class guys. Every-one I knew liked Mr. Sullivan, but I hadn't realized his popularity extended this far—there was a small cohort of cheerleaders, and two seniors from the football team. I sat near Rogan and several of our friends in the third row. Mr. Sullivan sat in the very front, by himself, with a notebook, a script, and several mimeographed sheets of dialogue.

I assumed Rogan and I would be permitted to audition together. Instead, Mr. Sullivan had all the girls read, one at a time, and then all the boys. The girls were given the same two speeches of Olivia's. In the first, Olivia declared her love for the boy Cesario—actually Viola in disguise—while in the second Olivia berated her drunken uncle Toby, and then fawned over Sebastian, Viola's twin brother, thinking he was Cesario. I listened, and secretly gloated, as the cheerleaders stumbled over the strange words and meanings.

"Mr. Sullivan, this is confusing!" one of them wailed.

"Imagine how confusing it is to Lady Olivia," said Mr. Sullivan.

My turn came. A moonfaced girl with long flaxen hair walked off the stage and handed me a script. I glanced at Rogan.

"Break a leg," he said.

Onstage, a row of lights shone down blindingly. I shielded my eyes and stared out into the auditorium, but could see only vague smears and shadows. Was that Mr. Sullivan? Rogan? When I looked down, the white pages of my script glowed with a diabolical brilliance.

"Whenever you're ready, Madeline."

I nodded and smiled nervously.

"O, what a deal of scorn looks beautiful
In the contempt and anger of his lip!"

"Louder," said Mr. Sullivan.

I cleared my throat and began again.

"O, what a deal of scorn looks beautiful
In the contempt and anger of his lip!
A murd'rous guilt shows not itself more soon
Than love that would seem hid. Love's night is noon."

The cheerleader was right: it made no sense. My face burned. The words of Olivia's speech began to skitter across the page like insects fleeing a light. I took a deep breath and concentrated on speaking as clearly as I could, on getting through the speech without passing out. When I was finished, I stumbled from the stage and thrust the pages at the next girl, then collapsed into the seat beside Rogan.

"That was horrible," I gasped.

Rogan grinned. "You did great."

The boys' auditions weren't much more impressive than the girls'. Mr. Sullivan gave them the speech that opens the play, Duke Orsino's command, "If music be the food of love, play on!" Their second reading was cobbled together from Orsino's amatory advice to Cesario.

I was disconcerted by how good the two football players sounded, though maybe it was just that their booming voices were more suited to the Duke's admonitory tone. Or maybe it was simply that anything sounded better than my own dismal effort had.

"Rogan?" Mr. Sullivan pointed at my cousin. "You ready?"

Rogan shook his head. "I'm going last."

I looked at him furtively. He was taller than me, of course, but then, Viola's twin brother would have been taller than she was. Our eyes were different colors, but would anyone be able to tell that from the audience?

The main thing was the hair. But surely I could find a wig among Madeline's trappings or in the box of props and costumes stored in a closet at St. Brendan's. Or Mr. Sullivan would buy one.

"Okay, Rogan," said Mr. Sullivan. "You're up."

Rogan went onstage. He moved around, face turned to the light, until he found a spot he liked; then began to read.

"If music be the food of love, play on!
Give me excess of it that, surfeiting,
The appetite may sicken and so die . . ."

I watched, transfixed. Everyone did.

Because Rogan didn't pronounce the words in a fake English accent or stumble as though they were a foreign language. He read them as though he knew what he was saying. And when it seemed like maybe he didn't, he winged it—he mimed some other, private meaning, looking slyly sideways at the audience and indicating by a gesture or smile that, even if we didn't understand what was going on, *he* did.

Only we *did* understand. I did, anyway, and when I stole a look at the other students, I saw that they did, too. They laughed or stared at Rogan with this odd expression of delight and disbelief, as though they'd just been told school was canceled for the day.

Only Mr. Sullivan didn't seem surprised. He leaned back in his seat, chin in hand and a small, knowing smile on his face, as Rogan straightened and began the Duke's second speech.

"Come hither, boy. If ever thou shalt love,
In the sweet pangs of it remember me . . ."

When he reached the end, Rogan tossed the script pages into the audience, made a mocking bow, and jumped offstage. There were murmurs of approval, and then everyone began to clap and cheer.

"Thank you, Rogan," said Mr. Sullivan, as he'd said to everyone. He looked pleased, but also businesslike. "Thank you all. I'll post the cast list first thing Monday morning."

"Monday?" I said in dismay. "We have to wait till Monday?"

Mr. Sullivan nodded. "Yup. Have a good weekend, everybody."

Several people clustered around Rogan as we left the auditorium.

"Hey, man, that was good." One of the football players pretended to punch Rogan's arm. "Play on!"

"You were really funny." The flaxen-haired girl smiled, then turned to me. "You were good, too, Maddy. See you Monday."

On the way home, I found myself looking at Rogan warily. It was like the day his voice had changed, when I'd first heard him sing in a chilling tenor that had come from—where? The same place this ability to act Shakespeare had come from, obviously.

But when had he learned this? *Had* he learned it? Or was it some bizarre fluke, like his voice?

"Did you—did you practice that?" I finally asked him.

"Practice? Yeah, some." He reached into his pocket and took out a pack of cigarettes, glanced around, then lit one. "I read it in front of the mirror in my room. Isn't that what you did?"

"Yeah," I said. But I was lying.

I looked at him again and thought of what Aunt Kate had said about glamour. That it could be taught, and learned. That it wasn't a matter of magic or luck.

"You were better than me," I said at last. "A lot better."

❖ ❖ ❖

ON MONDAY I WENT TO SCHOOL EARLY. ROGAN
liked to sleep until the last possible second, so I walked up by myself.
None of the buses had arrived yet, and only a few of the teachers. I
looked for Mr. Sullivan's Dodge Dart but didn't see it in the parking
lot. Inside I dumped my stuff in my locker, then with feigned non-
chalance strolled to the English Department. The bulletin board was
empty, save for an outdated announcement about the school poetry
magazine.

I killed time as best I could, drifting around the library where I
read old magazines. When I went back to the English Department, a
knot of people was crowded around the bulletin board. One of them
was Rogan.

"Maddy." He gave me a strained look. "You got your part."

"Really?"

He pointed at the cast list. I slipped through the crowd to stand
beside him, and scanned the names on the typesheet.

TWELFTH NIGHT CAST

ORSINO, Duke of Illyria   Kevin Hayes
VIOLA, a shipwrecked lady   Madeline Tierney
SEBASTIAN, twin brother of Viola   Duncan Moss

My mouth went dry. Duncan Moss was a nondescript sopho-more with longish brown hair and glasses. He was standing in the crowd, too, and flashed me a happy grin.

Short, I thought with a sick feeling; he was short and had hair the same color as mine. Onstage, without makeup or wigs, we'd look alike.

"Oh. Jeez." I turned to Rogan. "Did you—?"

He gave me a twisted, I-told-you-so smile, then jabbed his thumb at the final name on the list.

FESTE, a clown also called FOOL, Olivia's jester

Rogan Tierney

"Typecasting," he said. He turned and walked away.

Our first rehearsal was that afternoon. We sat in chairs onstage, where Mr. Sullivan handed each of us a new Penguin paperback edi-tion of the play.

"You can make whatever notes you like in these," he said.

"You mean, like, we can write in the book?" asked Duncan Moss.

"I think it would be a very good idea," said Mr. Sullivan.

We all smiled tentatively. Rogan took out a pen and made a big X on the cover of his paperback. Mr. Sullivan shot him an admonitory look.

"Hey, I'm the fool," said Rogan guilelessly, and everyone laughed.

"The zanies have their own little world, outside the mundane one that we live in, that Olivia and Orsino live in," said Mr. Sullivan later. It was too soon to start any blocking, but he stood and paced the stage, tracing an invisible boundary. "It's not governed by our laws—that's what the holiday of Twelfth Night is all about, a time when the Lord of Misrule takes over and our world is turned upside down. For the play to work, the audience has to completely believe in that other world. They have to look at Viola disguised as a boy named Cesario, and see a boy there, the same boy Olivia is in love with. But they also have to see Viola."

Abruptly he stopped and looked at me expectantly. I gazed at my script, flustered.

"Methinks she is speechless," said Rogan, and everyone laughed again.

"It's a balancing act," said Mr. Sullivan. "Acting is a matter of balance. Method actors, they say they lose themselves in a part—but you don't really want to lose yourself, do you?"

I looked up. Mr. Sullivan was still staring at me.

"Because if you really lost yourself," he said in a low voice, "you might not come back."

We finished the read-through, and Mr. Sullivan slapped his book against his knee. "Good job, everyone. We'll meet every day right after school, this week and next. After that we'll start going into night rehearsals."

We all stood to go. Rogan gathered his books and joined me.

"I don't know how you're going to balance *those*." He gazed pointedly down my uniform blouse. "Master Cesario."

"Rogan." Mr. Sullivan came up behind us. "Can you read music?"

"Not really. I fool around with the guitar, but—no."

"That's all right. Here." Mr. Sullivan pulled something from his briefcase and handed it to Rogan. "I want you to listen to this. All the songs marked *Feste*? I want you to learn them."

"Thanks," said Rogan, bemused.

It was a record album titled *Songs from Shakespeare*, illustrated with a dreary-looking bust of Shakespeare. Rogan turned to the back cover. There was a boring description of antique musical instruments, followed by a long list of songs, with play titles and character names beside them.

"Hey." Rogan looked at Mr. Sullivan in surprise. "This is a lot of music."

I peered over his shoulder. The entire second side of the album was taken up with songs from *Twelfth Night*, all of them sung by Feste.

Mr. Sullivan nodded. "It's a part for a singer. A strong singer. See what you can do with it."

He put a hand on Rogan's shoulder and smiled. "I've heard you singing by yourself in your room. I'd like you to sing like that here—"

He gestured at the empty auditorium. "When all those seats are full. Think you can do it?"

Rogan shrugged. "Yeah, sure. I guess."

We walked home. It was too late for us to steal any time alone, so we said good night in the street in front of my house.

"What do you think?" I asked.

"I dunno. I was kind of bummed at first. But now . . ." He glanced at the record album. "I guess I'll see how this music sounds."

I stood and waited for him to say something about me, about the different voices I'd tried using as Viola—one for when she was a girl, the other for when she was dressed as Cesario. But he just stared at the record.

"Well," he said at last. "I better go put this on. See you."

I had trouble falling asleep that night. I read and reread the play—my scenes, anyway—and tried to make sense of the unfamiliar words and the scrawled notes I'd made of Mr. Sullivan's commentary. In act 3, Viola and the Fool had a scene together. I read her part aloud.

"So thou mayst say the king lies by a beggar if a beggar dwell near him, or the church stands by thy tabor if thy tabor stand by the church."

I frowned and deciphered my scribbled notes.

Tabor = drum

I tried to imagine Rogan speaking his lines and me responding.

"I warrant thou art a merry fool and carest for nothing."

It was hopeless. I dropped the book and turned off the light, lay in the dark, and thought of Rogan. It felt like weeks since we'd been together in the attic. I tried to dredge up an image of the toy theater, the eerie dance of light upon its arches and tiny stage; I tried to recall Rogan's voice, singing, and imagine his hands on me and not my own.

But it didn't work, any of it. I was alone. The room was silent and dark. I could no more fill it with Rogan's face or voice or touch than

I could fill it with snow or rain. I had no glamour, no magic; no voice to summon up anything extraordinary, here or onstage.

I had no presence.

I brooded on why Mr. Sullivan had even cast me as Viola. Anna, the flaxen-haired girl, was prettier and at least as good an actress as I was—why hadn't he chosen her?

The only reason I could come up with was that Duncan Moss and I could, in a pinch, at a distance, pass for twins.

That was it. There was no glamour in it. No talent, even. Just cold necessity.

I shivered. I felt light-headed and shaken, as when I first saw the toy theater. I stared at the dark ceiling and remembered Aunt Kate's words.

It's something that can be taught. It can be learned. Words, how to speak and walk. How to make your voice carry. Diction . . .

I thought of Rogan, how effortless it was for him. All he had to do was say the lines, and people laughed.

The tail wags the dog with him.

I couldn't do that. I was too self-conscious; people would never look at me of their own accord.

But maybe I could *make* them look at me.

You're building a house, a beautiful house, a little bit at a time out of all these things.

I thought of how Rogan moved, of his hands drawing patterns in the air. I thought of how he walked, shoulders canted back slightly, head tilted as though he were trying to listen to some far-off sound. His face raised always to the light; the way he'd stare at you so intently it was like a challenge, even if he said nothing. You take all these little things and you build a house. You build a character, a shell, and if you build it right, something comes to live inside it.

Olivia wasn't in love with Viola. She was in love with a make-believe boy that the grief-stricken Viola had created from the memory of her drowned twin.

"Well, I'll put it on, and I will dissemble myself in't," Feste says as he disguises himself to torment poor Malvolio. *"I would I were the first that ever dissembled in such a gown . . . The competitors enter."*

I might not possess glamour; I might not be a magician.

But I could learn to be a good carpenter.

And I could learn to be a thief. I reached for my copy of the script, turned the light back on, and began once more to read.

The competitors enter.

❖ ❖ ❖

IT WAS LESS LIKE BUILDING A HOUSE THAN COLO-nizing an island, this freakish, lovely, marvelous atoll that rose from the gray wasteland of St. Brendan's High School like some extravagant Atlantis we'd willed into being. All of our previous alliances and identities were tossed aside—jock, freak, egghead, cheerleader, anonymous.

But who or what we became wasn't necessarily reflected by the parts we played in *Twelfth Night*. It really was as if we were castaways, our place in Illyria determined as much by luck and skill—and not necessarily acting ability—as by a shared determination to make the play a success. It was my first full-bore exposure to the virus that is theater, not just watching a show but becoming part of its chemistry, the intricate helices of desire and ambition and love and unrelenting effort involved in producing even a bad play. And we all realized, almost from the very beginning, that our *Twelfth Night* was going to be remarkable.

For one thing, everyone knew their lines in record time. This in itself was unusual—apart from Rogan and myself, the cast had only the most rudimentary prior knowledge of Shakespeare. It really *was* like a virus: the boy playing Sir Toby caught it from Olivia, and Sebastian caught it from me, and Sir Andrew caught it from Maria—you get the picture. In the middle of a rehearsal, an actor would stride onstage and abruptly, as though he or she had been pumped with speed, start riffing on the lines.

Sudden meaning tumbled out of seemingly banal or incomprehensible exchanges. Malvolio pulled double and triple entendres from his famous scene with the forged love letter. Olivia didn't just come on to my Viola disguised as Cesario: she began to look suggestively at Maria, too. Backstage, Sir Toby would grab on to one of the heavy ropes that controlled the curtain, twist it around as though he were a kid on a swing, then spin himself dizzy, letting go at the last moment to stagger onstage for his scene in such a convincing display of drunkenness that Mr. Sullivan once checked his breath to make sure he hadn't smuggled a bottle backstage. Sir Andrew and Sebastian engaged in such extended swordplay that by opening night both were covered with cuts and bruises.

As for Feste—well, if there was a Patient Zero in this epidemic, it was Rogan. He didn't just learn his lines with a facility that was unnerving. As with the audition, he somehow intuited what they meant and made the meaning clear to everyone who heard him.

And then there were his songs. At rehearsal a few days after Mr. Sullivan had given him the album of Shakespeare's music, Rogan returned it to him.

Mr. Sullivan frowned. "Did you listen to it?"

"Yeah, I listened to it."

"And?"

Rogan gave him an odd half smile. "It was interesting."

Mr. Sullivan's mouth was tight as he slid the album back into his briefcase. "Places, everyone," he called.

The opening scenes went well, though not spectacularly so.

And then Feste made his first entrance, with Maria.

"O mistress mine, where are you roaming?"

The line was from later in the play—a song, according to the script, though Rogan had only ever spoken the lines in rehearsal. Now he sang them.

We heard him before we saw him, that soaring voice like something you'd hear in a dream or a church or a movie, so high and clear and utterly unexpected that there was muffled laughter, followed by surprised gasps as Rogan walked onstage.

Because of course we'd all heard him sing before, in church or just goofing around at school. But no one, not even me, had ever heard anything like this. He only sang two lines, the sweet falsetto at odds with the feline way he walked, and with his expression as he looked past Maria to where I stood offstage.

"O stay and hear, your true love's coming . . ."

I tore my gaze from him to look at Mr. Sullivan, seated as usual in the first row. He stared at Rogan blissfully, almost stoned with delight. So, by the end of rehearsal, did everyone else.

I've seen spectacular performances since then—Anthony Hopkins's Broadway debut in *Equus*, Kevin Kline in *On the Twentieth Century*, John Wood in *The Invention of Love*. Rogan's turn as the Clown rivaled all of them.

Everyone in that auditorium felt it: everyone was bewitched. I felt drugged, light-headed with desire and raw adrenaline. Whatever envy I had burned away at the expectation of sharing the stage with him. It was like sex—it *was* sex, magnified somehow and transformed into a vision we could all see, all share in; and there was Rogan, grinning and looking as happy as I'd ever seen him outside of the hidden space in his room.

From that moment on, the production was charmed. Malvolio, who was wonderful to begin with, became a miracle of cunning and pathos and self-love. The pallid, flaxen-haired Olivia was a bombshell. Duncan Moss as Sebastian grew dashing and began to flirt with me. Even the members of the tech club, the usually dour collective of outcasts who toiled at sound and lights and props and costumes, rose to the occasion with uncharacteristic displays of exuberance, going so far as to applaud scenes they'd watched a hundred times.

We all were good. But we took our cues from Rogan. There was a subtle undercurrent to everything Feste said, everything he sang; as if he knew some other, deeper, secret meaning attached to the play, something strange, even supernatural; something the rest of us could never hope to understand, although we drove ourselves crazy trying to.

Especially me.

"Would not a pair of these have bred, sir?" Rogan held up a quarter, the payment I'd given Feste so that he'd let Viola pass Olivia's gates.

"Yes, being kept together and put to use," I retorted.

But before I could push my way past him, he sidled up beside me and kissed me, his mouth lingering so that I felt his tongue between my lips.

I stumbled backward, mortified. Offstage someone laughed.

"I would play Lord Pandarus of Phrygia, sir," Rogan went on, *"to bring a Cressida to this Troilus."*

"That's great, Maddy!" Mr. Sullivan called from his seat in the audience. "Brilliant, Rogan!"

Several of Malvolio's big scenes came soon after this, and neither Rogan nor I was on for a while. I found him backstage and dragged him behind the fire curtain.

"Are you nuts?" I hissed.

"Yes," he whispered. He drew me to him and kissed me again, harder, pulling me so close I could feel his heart pound. "Maddy . . ."

I trembled so much it hurt to speak. "Rogan—stop. I have to go on."

"My parents are gone tonight. Michael's going to Derek's. Come over afterward."

I nodded, turned, and stumbled off to make my entrance.

That night, lying with Rogan in the attic, I felt nearly delirious with arousal, and what I now know was pure, unchecked joy. I knew it then, too; knew that whatever happiness lay in store for me—vast continents of happiness, I was certain, of which this was only the first glimpse of shore—this would always be what I remembered. My cousin beside me, the toy theater's radiance lapping our bodies in waves of gold and green while phantom lightning flickered in Rogan's eyes and phantom vapor roiled across the tiny stage, all those rustlings and whispers silenced by Rogan's voice, singing softly beside me in the dark.

> *"When that I was and a little tiny boy,*
> *With hey, ho, the wind and the rain,*
> *A foolish thing was but a toy,*
> *For the rain it raineth every day."*

He turned to me and stroked my cheek. "I love you, Maddy."

"I love you, too," I whispered.

It was the first time we had ever spoken it aloud.

It was now the week before Christmas. The show was scheduled to open on January 6, the real Twelfth Night. Everyone connected with the play was practically incandescent with excitement and expectation. The corridors at St. Brendan smelled of roses and burned sugar; the overhead lights hummed with a scintillant, cracked-ice glow. I felt as though I were walking around inside the toy theater; as though it had grown, like the magical stage tree in *The Nutcracker*, to encompass everyone I knew, everything I touched.

On Christmas Eve, the last day of school before Christmas break, and after a rehearsal that went on into the night, we exchanged gifts backstage.

Funny gifts, mostly. Duncan Moss gave me an athletic supporter. Maria furtively slipped Sir Toby a pint of rum. Sir Andrew and I exchanged plastic swords. Mr. Sullivan told us we were all exempted from taking the English exam scheduled for when classes resumed.

"Where's Rogan?" he asked.

I looked around. "He was just here—"

Rogan suddenly materialized, stepping from the shadows onto the stage. "Maddy," he called. "Catch!"

I turned and got hit in the face by a snowball. "Hey!"

"Oops," said Rogan. His face was flushed as he pointed to the fire door. "Everyone! Come here, look—"

We ran to the door, then streamed outside, laughing and shouting in amazement.

"It's snowing!"

None of us had ventured from the auditorium for hours. When school ended, the sky had been gray and the ground barren.

Now a good six inches covered Mr. Sullivan's car and drifted up against the sides of the building and into the unplowed streets beyond. The air was so thick with snow I couldn't tell who stood beside me, Olivia or Sebastian or one of the guys from the tech club.

"Maddy," came a voice at my ear. It was Rogan. He made a slow backward pratfall, until he lay on his back in a snowdrift, grinning like a lunatic. "Merry Christmas."

❖ ❖ ❖

THAT YEAR, FOR THE FIRST TIME, CHRISTMAS
seemed anticlimactic. The usual buzz around the Arden Terrace hive
was muted. A lot of the older cousins didn't come home or made
only fleeting visits. There was no one younger than Rogan or myself
to spur parents to keep up the pretenses of the season, and all the
adults seemed more tired, less interested in the holiday than usual:
exhausted but also relieved that they didn't have to make the long slog
through the Valley of the Shadow of Santa Claus. Mr. Sullivan hadn't
called any rehearsals until a few days after Christmas, but the break
didn't feel like a treat. It felt like an exile. Not even the modest, but still
impressive, pile of presents with my name on them cheered me up,
until I got to the large box from Aunt Kate.

"This isn't a new present, Maddy." She sat in the wing chair in our
living room, having made the rounds of the other families since early
that morning. As usual, we were last on her roster; as usual, she took
the whiskey sour my father gave her and sipped it as my sisters and I
opened our gifts. "But at least this time I know that it fits."

I opened it, suspicious of the Gimbels logo on the box, then
gasped.

"Oh, Aunt Kate." I drew it out, the midnight folds falling about
me and exhaling a faint fragrance of camphor and Chanel No. 5 and
roses. "Thank you, thank you so much . . ."

My mother asked, "Is that Madeline's old cape?"

"It is." Aunt Kate sipped her whiskey and watched me. "I took it out of storage a while ago and had it cleaned. I knew it fit—Maddy's worn it before—but I wanted to be sure she'd take good care of it."

"I will," I said as my sisters looked on, unsure whether they should be jealous or not. "You know I will."

Aunt Kate nodded. Her blue agate eyes narrowed.

"You'd better," she said.

A few days later we went back to rehearsing; a few days after that school began once more. I hadn't seen Aunt Kate and Mr. Sullivan together for some time, not since we'd all gone down to the city to see *Jumpers*.

During that last week of rehearsals, she showed up every afternoon. She sat in the very back of the auditorium, where the Tech Club guys hung out when they weren't needed. They had started out as a nerdy bunch, but as the weeks passed a sea change had overtaken them, as well. They started getting high with Rogan in the parking lot before school; they let their hair grow long and began listening to different music. *Tales from Topographic Oceans* gave way to *Transformer* and *Electric Warrior*. The first time I saw Aunt Kate in their midst I felt a stab of panic—embarrassment at having an adult family member intrude upon our hidden world; fear that from this vantage point she'd see the indelible path charting my fall from grace, from earnest, slightly anonymous niece to pot-smoking infidel and incestuous wanton.

But she said nothing. And the tech guys seemed to like her.

Sometimes she'd slip from her row to join Mr. Sullivan, her high heels ticking softly until she sank into the seat beside him. If I were onstage, I'd try not to get flustered, seeing them with their heads together, whispering. If I were backstage I'd peer from behind the curtains and vainly try to decipher what they were saying. Were they happy with the box tree scene? Did Malvolio caper too gaily in his cross-gartered yellow stockings?

Mostly they seemed to focus on Rogan. Mr. Sullivan would lean back, pencil at his lips, with the same stoned smile he had every time my cousin sang. Aunt Kate's expression was more difficult to read: tight-mouthed, keen-eyed, unsmiling; but was it disapproval or sheer amazement?

It could have been either. And I was afraid to ask.

Rogan didn't seem to care. It was all one to him: if the auditorium was empty or if a few parents and students wandered in to watch, if we were in costume or still wore our uniforms, if someone else missed a cue, or if the followspot failed to pick him out from the darkness. Rogan moved and sang and spoke as though it was always opening night.

Until, at last, it was.

On Thursday, we had a spectacularly botched final run-through, upholding the old superstition that a bad dress rehearsal portends a successful show. Sir Toby blew his lines and improvised with a series of obscene couplets and Firesign Theater routines. Andrew Aguecheek's sword poked me squarely in the stomach, knocking the wind from me so I couldn't finish the scene. An amber gel on a followspot melted and the stage reeked of charred plastic. Olivia giggled uncontrollably through her love scenes. I forgot my lines, not once but over and over again. The entire rehearsal felt like the quintessential Actor's Nightmare.

That night Aunt Kate was *not* in the audience, an absence that should have been a relief but instead struck me as slightly ominous. Rogan sang his final song, "Hey, ho, the wind and the rain," and the stage at last went dark. Mr. Sullivan made us practice a curtain call, and this, too, made me uneasy.

"Don't worry," he assured us. "Tomorrow it will be fine. You'll see. Now everyone go and get a good night's sleep."

Olivia looked stricken. "Don't you have any notes?"

"Yeah," said Rogan. "Tomorrow night, don't fuck up."

Mr. Sullivan smiled. "Get some sleep. Rogan, give your voice a rest. No Rolling Stones, okay? And no cigarettes."

"Yeah, sure," said Rogan.

Outside, in the school parking lot, no one hung around. Mr. Sullivan had already left. The tech guys stayed to clean up the mess left by the burned gel. Toby and Olivia and Fabian and Malvolio and Maria all clambered into Toby's car to get dropped off at their respective homes. Duncan Moss's father picked him up as he always did, along with a few other grumpy-looking parents—the dress rehearsal had run even later than usual.

Rogan and I walked home together. He still wore Feste's makeup, a Pierrot mask of white with two crimson spots on his cheeks. The red had rubbed away from his mouth, but the kohl around his eyes remained, smudged so that his eyes seemed enormous, like those of some nocturnal frog or bush baby. He looked beautiful and deeply, strangely androgynous; unearthly, almost inhuman.

"We should have gotten a ride," I said, shivering.

The previous week's snow had turned into a gunmetal soup of

slush and ice. The air was clear and so bitingly cold that Christmas lights and traffic lights and street lamps all seemed to shiver and dance, even though there was no wind. The smoke from Rogan's cigarette clung to us long after he'd tossed the cigarette aside. As we approached Arden Terrace his hand found mine and held it, tightly.

"It'll go well," he said in a soft voice. His hand felt as though it had been carved from granite. "It'll be great, Maddy."

"It'll be the first time we're onstage together," I said. I felt my heart open at the thought. "Everyone will see us. Everyone will hear you."

"They've already heard me," said Rogan.

"But not like this."

"No," he said, and turning to me he smiled.

It was like my own reflection in a black mirror, only a mirror that stripped the flesh from my skull so that what grinned back was not the self I showed the daytime world, not the girl who woke and walked and struggled and laughed but the terrible me, the true me; the mad girl inside Maddy. I stared back at him but said nothing, only clutched his hand even tighter, until it felt as though his fingers cut into mine. For the first time in years, I thought of the word Aunt Kate had always used to describe him—*fey*—and my mother's blunt retort.

If I ever had a red-headed child, I'd strangle it.

"Maddy."

He stopped in the street in front of my house and put his arms around me. Even through our jeans and heavy coats I could feel his cock pressing into my groin. I shut my eyes and tried to summon snow, the icy glitter of footlights, and a sun the size of a thumbprint through pink and amber clouds.

But all I saw was ash and a tangle of broken masts, and all I tasted was smoke, a warm spurt of salt where Rogan's chapped lip split beneath mine and blood stained both our mouths until he pulled away, laughing, and walked down the darkened path toward Fairview.

❖ ❖ ❖

THE HOUSE WAS THREE-QUARTERS FULL FOR OPENing night. My parents were there, and Rogan's; two of my sisters and his brother Michael, as well as Aunt Kate and a thin scattering of aunts and uncles. Aunt Kate had dressed as though we were making our Broadway debut, in her lizard-skin boots and a beautiful, embroidered Russian peasant skirt and blouse of jade-green silk. She sat a few rows behind Mr. Sullivan, near a group of St. Brendan's staff, her hands demurely crossed in her lap and her emerald ring casting a green flare from the overhead lights. There were other parents, of course, and numerous children, siblings of the other cast members; as well as students.

Not just the usual Drama Club boosters, either: there was an impressive, rather intimidating block of football players and assorted jocks, as well as cheerleaders, JV and Varsity, and even a few kids from the local public school.

"Shit!" said Orsino. His eyes had the wild white gleam of a spooked horse's, but he sounded exhilarated. "Look at these people!"

I gritted my teeth and gestured at him to shut up. I was doing my best *not* to look at anyone. I stood just offstage and stared resolutely at the ropes and suspended weights that held backdrops and curtains in place. I'd peeked out earlier and seen the audience, and now I could hear them, along with the excited whispers and muffled laughter of the other actors around me. I felt so sick I thought I might pass out. I *wanted* to pass out, even though that would mean the show would be canceled.

I no longer cared. The horror I felt every time I looked at the stage, that brightly lit array of furniture and fake shrubs and cardboard scenery, was so intense it overpowered any other emotion.

"Hey, Maddy. You ready?" One of the boys who handled the curtains looked at me in concern. I nodded. "You sure?"

I took a step backward and knocked against the sand-filled canister that was a safeguard against fires; then bent and vomited into it.

"Uh, guess not." The boy grimaced. He pushed the can out of the way and grabbed one of the ropes. A minute later I heard the stage manager's voice.

"Places, everyone."

I wiped my mouth and looked across the stage. In the shadows stood Rogan, clad in his loose white Pierrot tunic and pantaloons, his feet bare, hair a loose halo around a ghostly face. He was singing to himself, soundlessly, staring at the stage floor and moving as though he saw his reflection there and danced with it. After a moment he glanced up and saw me. Very slowly he raised his fingers to his lips and kissed them, then extended his hand to me, palm forward. His head sank to his breast as though he had fallen asleep, so all I saw was that cloud of fiery hair.

"... lights and—*curtain.*"

I waited, mouth dry, through Orsino's opening scene, the welcoming wave of laughter as he paced the stage with a golf club and knocked over the plastic geraniums, one by one. He seemed less lovesick than drug addled.

But the scene worked, just as it had in rehearsal. Better, even.

And faster. Before I could blink, Orsino exited, giddy from the scattered applause that followed him. The lights darkened to red and indigo. Someone shook a thunder sheet. A spotlight flickered. The Captain walked on, a tall blond jock who looked like a rock star in his pseudo-naval costume, along with two sailors. They took their places front and center and gazed expectantly at me in the wings. I drew a shuddering breath and raked my fingers through my hair, then stumbled on to fall at the Captain's feet and gaze up at him imploringly.

"*What country, friends, is this?*"

"*This is Illyria, lady.*" The Captain looked past me, to where Rogan stood offstage.

"*And what should I do in Illyria?*" I turned to stare at my cousin, and began to cry. "*My brother, he is in Elysium . . .*"

I recall almost nothing else of my performance, though I remembered all my lines, all my entrances. People applauded when I walked offstage. They laughed at the right places. I took my pratfalls during my duel with Sir Andrew and praised the countess so that the very babbling gossip of the air cried out "Olivia."

But it was like being stone-cold drunk in a darkened room. Only when Rogan was on did the stage suddenly seem to shake and blaze, as though lightning struck it: his flaming hair, his white costume irradiated by the followspots, his bare feet kicking up a shining haze of dust and rouge and face powder that followed him like a bright shadow. When he first opened his mouth and sang I heard a gasp go through the audience, as though everyone had at the same instant touched a burning wire.

Then the house fell silent.

It was as though I were alone in the attic. Only now, the toy theater had grown to the size of a real one. I watched my cousin, his slender form pacing in front of the footlights, the scrim behind him backlit so I could see the faintest suggestion of tree limbs and the outlines of a wrecked ship, the moon rising above distant mountains, and the blue shadows of the other actors. His voice echoed from the rafters, so piercing and full of heartbreak I felt as if that burning wire had been thrust into my skull. When he finished, he stepped backward and gave a small, plaintive bow, then straightened as, slowly at first, then with the sudden irrevocable rush of water flooding a broken building, the place erupted into applause.

"Holy fuck," someone behind me breathed.

I couldn't speak. I stood beside the curtain and peeked out into the audience.

People were still applauding—jocks, mostly, all fired up with the beer they'd snuck into the auditorium. I saw Mr. Sullivan with Sister Mary Clark beside him, whispering in his ear. A few rows behind them were my parents and sister, who seemed to have reverted to some sort of racial memory of how to behave at the theater. They held their mimeographed programs and clapped and appeared enthusiastic, if bemused: as though they'd suddenly awakened here, fully dressed, and were trying very hard not to draw attention to themselves.

But Rogan's mother looked strained and unsure how to react. I saw her glance furtively at the people sitting next to her, who beamed and nodded, while Aunt Pat kept her hands poised just above her lap.

Meanwhile, Rogan's father stared stony-eyed at the stage, not even looking at Rogan but beyond him, as though someone else were to blame for what he'd just witnessed. My skin prickled and I took a step backward, then told myself that was stupid, there was no way he could see me through the curtain. I continued to search the audience until I found Aunt Kate.

"Don't miss your cue," someone hissed at me.

I nodded but didn't move. My mouth went dry; I felt as I had in those terrible moments before the curtains first parted.

Because Aunt Kate was weeping. Not wiping at the corners of her eyes, as I'd seen her do during a performance of *King Lear*, or crying demurely as she did at a sad movie, or even staring stoic and wet faced as she did at Tierney funerals.

Now she was bent almost double as her body heaved with sobs. Even from backstage I could see how her face had gone dead white. Her eyes and mouth were red slits, like the openings in a mask. She looked as though she were having a seizure or a heart attack; but before I could move, the stage manager grabbed my arm and pushed me toward the stage.

"For chrissakes, you're *on!*"

It was all a blur after that. Love scene, swordplay, mad scene, reconciliation: all flickered around me, a slide show glimpsed through a fever dream—until the play's last moments.

Everyone exited, save Feste. He stood alone, the stage dark except for a single thin followspot that picked out his face: the white makeup smudged, the rouge gone from his cheeks and lips. Only his eyes were more brilliant than ever, blazing aquamarine as he tilted his chin toward the light and sang.

"When that I was and a little tiny boy,
With hey, ho, the wind and the rain,
A foolish thing was but a toy,
For the rain it raineth every day."

I stood with everyone else backstage and watched. Our curtain calls were forgotten, the audience was forgotten. Rogan himself was gone. There was only song and light, and the dust swirling around him in a nimbus of gold and black. As though he'd given voice to it; as though he'd given voice to all of us, and we would flicker back into darkness when he fell silent.

"But when I came, alas, to wive,
With hey, ho, the wind and the rain,
By swaggering could I never thrive,
For the rain it raineth every day."

I didn't know I was crying, until Malvolio gasped and pulled me to him. Dimly I grew aware of other sounds backstage, muffled sobs and breathing. Someone else put their hands on my shoulders. Not to comfort me; more the way a scared child reaches for an adult in the night.

"A great while ago the world begun,
With hey, ho, the wind and the rain,
But that's all one, our play is done,
And we'll strive to please you every day."

The followspot wavered as Rogan raised his hands. His eyes closed as the last notes echoed through the house. The spotlight went out; the auditorium plunged into darkness. His voice hung there still. I shut my eyes and felt him beside me, felt his mouth on mine and his breath warm against my cheek.

The lights went up in such a sudden blaze that everyone backstage started, then laughed nervously. I blinked and rubbed my eyes.

"Places for curtain call!"

The auditorium remained silent. Then, as the curtain parted, a roar of clapping and shouting and catcalls swept over us.

We all got our applause. Lovers, Puritan, knights and Captain and soldiers and attendants.

But it was Rogan's show. No one had ever doubted that, not since he'd first stepped onstage. He took one bow, then another; the curtains closed, then opened again, and we all ran back out for more calls. When the curtain closed for the last time, the drunken jocks chanted Rogan's name until he stepped out alone, front and center, his costume furred with dust and his golden hair wild around his white face.

He stared at the audience, elated, until someone put the house lights on. People shaded their eyes and looked around in confused delight. At last, they began to leave.

Onstage actors ran around breathlessly, kissing and embracing. Sir Andrew and Sebastian clashed swords as Maria and Olivia fell into each other's arms, laughing as they wept.

"*You were so good!*"

"*No,* you *were so good!*"

I went out front to receive congratulations from my parents.

"Very nice, very nice," my father said. He kissed me absently on the forehead. "Do you need a ride home?"

"No, there's a party, I'll get a ride later."

"You did very well, Maddy," said my mother, and she hugged me. "We're very proud of you."

I looked around for Rogan's parents. They stood stiffly with their son a few feet away, none of them talking, though it looked like I might have just missed something, an argument or maybe Rogan's announcement that he'd be at the after party.

"Maddy?"

I turned. Mr. Sullivan grinned at me, Aunt Kate at his side. "You were wonderful—you and Rogan both. Just super."

"Thanks."

"You did a lovely job, darling." Aunt Kate hugged me tightly, then kissed both of my cheeks. "And you—"

She reached out to take Rogan by the hand and pulled him to us. I had a glimpse of my uncle's face, gray and unflinching, before he turned and walked out of the auditorium. Mr. Sullivan grasped Rogan's shoulder.

"You were amazing, Rogan. Just incredible." Mr. Sullivan threw his head back and laughed. "That voice!"

Aunt Kate's nose wrinkled as she stared at the unlit cigarette in Rogan's hand. "That voice isn't going to last very long if Rogan doesn't take care of it."

She smiled; but there was no warmth in the way she gazed at Rogan, even as she ruffled his hair and added, "You gave a hundred percent out there tonight, darling."

His mouth twisted in a smile. "Two hundred percent."

Aunt Kate looked at him as though this were part of some other conversation. "Just make sure you save something for tomorrow, sweetheart," she said lightly. "And Sunday. You have two more performances."

Rogan shrugged. "Hey, I might not be here tomorrow. None of us might." He looked sideways at me and smiled. "You getting a ride with Dunc?"

I nodded.

"Come on, then." He bent to kiss Aunt Kate's cheek, then saluted Mr. Sullivan. "I'll see you tomorrow, Mr. S."

"No cigarettes!" Aunt Kate called after us. "Get a good night's sleep!"

The party was like Christmas, an anticlimax. Still, we all stayed till 3 A.M., getting high and passing around a gallon bottle of Almaden wine. Duncan Moss drove Rogan and me home, dropping us off at the top of Fairview's driveway.

"Fare well, my metal of India," Duncan said, and gave me a sloppy kiss.

"If he has an accident, you'll have to play Viola *and* Sebastian," said Rogan as we watched him drive off.

"Might be an improvement."

Rogan shook his head. "Nothing could be an improvement."

We stood with our arms wrapped around each other, swaying slightly while a moon just past full hung above the Hudson. Our breath formed a white cloud around us; underfoot a brittle layer of ice buckled and cracked.

"This is perfect," whispered Rogan. He buried his face in my hair and kissed my neck. "This, now—tonight—"

"Shhh," I said.

I knew what he was going to say next, knew it as though it were my own name. I kissed his mouth and silenced him, silenced everything except for the steady knocking of our chests, heart to heart, breath to breath, and the January wind blowing cold across Arden Terrace.

❖ ❖ ❖

THE AUDITORIUM HAD ONLY BEEN THREE-QUARTERS full on opening night. Saturday it was packed. The performance was even better than it had been the night before: word of mouth and repeat attendance by the jocks meant that Rogan's every entrance was met with cheers and whistles. He never lost his composure, though the other actors began to improvise, doing funny riffs and playing off the audience as though there were no fourth wall between us.

When the last act ended, Rogan received a standing ovation. He accepted it gracefully, beckoning the rest of us to join him onstage and saluting Mr. Sullivan where he sat, fifth row center, with Aunt Kate at his side. Afterward there was another party, a more formal affair thrown by Olivia's parents. Rogan didn't bother to change, but I wore my blue velvet cape. My father picked up Rogan and me before midnight.

"How did it go?" he asked as we climbed into the backseat.

"It went great," I said. Neither my parents nor Rogan's had come to the second performance. As far as I knew, they wouldn't attend the final one, either. "I'm tired, though."

"I'm not surprised." My father glanced at me in the rearview mirror. I thought he was going to say something, but he remained silent until after we dropped off Rogan.

"Aunt Kate came over this afternoon." He pulled the car into the garage and turned the ignition off, so we sat in darkness. "She wanted to talk to your mother and me about something."

He used the tone I'd always imagined a parent might use to announce a divorce or death.

"What?" My heart began to race. Had Aunt Kate blown the whistle on Rogan and me sleeping together? Did she even know? "Did something happen? Is it—"

"We'll talk about it tomorrow."

My father got out of the car. I stared after him, incredulous that he could drop this bomb but not watch it go off. "What do you mean, tomorrow? What happened? Is everyone okay?"

"Everyone's fine. Your mother and I will discuss it with you in the morning, I'm going to bed."

I spent an anxious night, finally resorted to taking a Valium Rogan had gotten from God knows where. Toward morning I fell asleep.

It was noon before I woke. That alone would have signaled that something was afoot—I had never been permitted to sleep that late, even when I was sick with chicken pox.

"Maddy?" I looked up blearily and saw my mother at the foot of my bed. "Aunt Kate's here. Why don't you get up and get dressed."

I took my time, showering and gathering everything I needed for the last show, a four o'clock matinee. If I'd even be allowed to perform in it. I wondered if Rogan had already had his meeting; if he was in my house right now, with Aunt Pat and Uncle Richard and my parents and Aunt Kate, all of them waiting to confront us.

But when I finally went downstairs, my parents and Aunt Kate were sitting cheerfully at the dining table, surrounded by coffee cups and half-finished plates of leftover turkey sandwiches.

"Good morning, Maddy," said Aunt Kate. "Did you get enough sleep?"

I looked at her uneasily. "I think so."

"Sit here, darling."

Aunt Kate pulled out the chair beside her. I sat, picked up a slice of pickle, and ate it.

"I came over yesterday to talk to your parents about something I've been working on for the last few months." Aunt Kate reached for the coffeepot and refilled her cup, held it in both hands so that the steam curled in gray wisps around her face. "I think it's time for you to go to London to study."

To hide my confusion, I took a sip of tepid coffee from someone else's cup. "Study what?"

"Acting. I've arranged for you to have an audition at the National Youth Theatre—they're still on their Christmas break. They rarely see potential students this time of year but I pulled some strings and they've agreed to meet with you. We'll have to get your passport photos immediately, but once that's taken care of we can go down to the city and just stand in line to have it processed. The main thing is that you need two audition pieces, one classical and one contemporary. You'll have to learn the contemporary one quickly. I think Lizzie in *The Rainmaker*. There's a good speech there; you'd do a super job with it."

I was still stuck back on that one word, *London*. "You mean England?"

"Yes." Aunt Kate exchanged a quick look with my parents.

"We'll leave you to discuss this," said my mother. She and my father stood, neither of them smiling, and left the room.

I stared at Aunt Kate, bewildered. She might as well have told me we were going to visit Middle-Earth or Mars.

"I don't get it," I said.

For a minute Aunt Kate sat and ran a finger across the face of her emerald ring.

"This is something I've given a great deal of thought to," she said at last. "And for a very long time. You're young, but your great-grandmother was younger than you when she first performed professionally. We can always dance around the age issue a bit if we have to—with the right makeup and clothes you could pass for seventeen. If you do well at the National Youth Theatre—and you will we can decide whether you should attend RADA or Central—Central School of Speech and Drama. But you'll be working well before then."

"I still don't—this is an acting school? In England?"

Aunt Kate nodded. "In London. I have old friends there. Some of them owe me a favor—not that you wouldn't be accepted on your own merits, but it never hurts to call in a favor."

I gaped at her in disbelief. "My parents—my parents know about this?"

Again she nodded. "I've already told them. I'll make all the arrangements, including tuition payment. And I'll stay with you, for the first few months anyway. I have a friend in Hampstead; we can use his flat while he's in Greece for the winter. After that we'll see what we can do. I have other friends. Highgate, maybe, or Belgravia."

"But." I stared at the table in front of me, the white cups and saucers and half-eaten sandwiches, then looked at my aunt. "Rogan."

Aunt Kate hesitated. "I can only afford tuition for one child."

"But Rogan." My mouth tasted bitter, as though I was going to be sick. "I mean—can't you take both of us?"

"No. Even if I wanted to, I can't afford it. And the school wouldn't look kindly on my taking advantage of them, asking to audition two students."

"But that's crazy." I shook my head so hard it hurt. "Rogan is— he's so much better. You know that, right? It's not just me who thinks so. Everyone does. Even Mr. Sullivan. Everyone!"

My voice rose. I began to cry. "You can't. It's not fair—you know it's not fair—"

"This has nothing to do with fair." Aunt Kate's tone was icy. She turned to avoid my gaze. "Rogan's a loose cannon. What he did in

Harlem that night—I'd be chasing all over London after him. His mother says he's taking drugs. And . . ."

She paused, staring at her hand. "There's very little they could teach him."

"What do you mean? He could do anything! You *know* that—"

Aunt Kate turned toward me. With one swift gesture she pulled the emerald ring from her finger.

"This was my grandmother's." Her voice shook as she thrust the ring within inches of my face. "This was Madeline Tierney's. She gave it to me for safekeeping. It has never belonged to me. Your cousin Rogan—"

She tilted the emerald until sunlight struck it and a green flare leaped from her fingers. Then she raised her hand and, with all her strength, threw the ring across the room. I cried out as it smashed into a cabinet, then dropped to the floor.

"Get it," said Aunt Kate. I shook my head and she repeated the command. "Get it and bring it to me, Madeline."

Crying, I stumbled to retrieve the ring and shoved it blindly at her. "No," she said.

She grabbed my hand and forced it open and placed the ring in my palm. When I looked down, I saw that the gold setting was damaged. The emerald was intact.

But it was no longer possible to wear the ring.

"It was a gift," said Aunt Kate. "A family heirloom. Just like his voice. You remember that, Madeline."

She stood. From the other room I heard my parents talking. The phone rang.

"Does he know?" I whispered.

"There was never a chance, Maddy. Not for a long time." Aunt Kate drew her hand to her face. Without the ring it seemed tiny, a child's hand and not a woman's. "But no, I haven't said anything to him. I think it would be better coming from you."

"I can't do that," I said. "How can you even think I could do that?"

Aunt Kate looked at me, her blue eyes bright with tears.

"You're an actor, Maddy." She turned to leave. "You'll find a way."

❖ ❖ ❖

I GRABBED MY THINGS AND FLED THE HOUSE through the back door, so I wouldn't have to face my parents. Rogan and I had planned to walk together to the last show.

But I was only halfway down his driveway when Fairview's front door opened and Rogan's brother Michael stepped out. He looked at me and shook his head, motioning for me to stop, then hurried up the drive to meet me.

"He's not here," he said. His face was flushed; he wore only a T-shirt and rubbed his arms to keep warm. "And if you were smart, you wouldn't be either."

"What? Is he okay? Where is he?"

"I don't know. He went over to Derek's a while ago for band practice. I guess he's still there."

"But—we have the last performance."

"Oh, he'll be there." Michael looked at me, his expression mingled disgust and fear. "Your precious show. You two should get some help, you know that? You should, anyway. *You're* not a total fucking idiot."

He turned and started back to the house.

"Wait—" I began, but Michael looked back and cut me off.

"Get out of here, Maddy," he said. "Now. Just go."

Rogan arrived backstage fifteen minutes before curtain time.

"Hey." He grabbed me and drew me close enough that I could smell marijuana and tobacco and mouthwash, then pulled away. "I got to get ready. See you in a few."

The house was full again. The performances—not just Rogan's, but mine, everyone's—were the best we'd ever done. My relief at not seeing any Tierneys in the audience was offset by the sight of Derek and some of his friends in the front row. I was afraid Rogan would leave with them afterward—our final cast party was supposed to be a wrap party, where we struck the sets.

Instead Derek and the other band members split right after the curtain calls. I couldn't blame them. It was ten minutes before we all stumbled offstage. I was elated despite myself, charged up from being onstage, from being in Rogan's orbit during our scenes together.

And, no matter that my stomach still churned at the thought, the phrase *London . . . I'm going to London* ran through my head like the opening lines of a speech I'd memorized. As I took my final bows, Orsino's hand in mine, I looked out at the audience on their feet and for a second shut my eyes, imagining another crowd there, another place; an outdoor theater, or an arena stage rather than a proscenium. Real acting teachers rather than Mr. Sullivan; real directors.

A real me, instead of the girl in scuffed tights and thrift shop costume, stepping back so that my cousin could take his customary bow, front and center.

When it was all finished, I changed quickly into the clothes I'd worn over, then looked for Rogan. I found him outside, smoking a cigarette in the brittle black air of early evening.

"Are you going to stay and help take everything down?" I asked.

He drew on his cigarette, then stubbed it out. "In a while. I'm going home first and get a sweater. I'm fucking freezing."

"Okay if I come?"

He grinned. "Sure, Mad-girl. Always."

We walked home. I knew I wouldn't be able to tell him in the secret attic or in his bedroom, or mine, just as I knew I couldn't tell him backstage. So I told him as we walked down the long hill toward Arden Terrace, shuffling through the dirty snow and gritty sand left by the plow trucks. As I spoke Rogan said nothing, only took out another cigarette and lit it, so I could see how his fingers trembled as he cupped the match between his hands.

"Wow," he said at last.

We were in the street in front of my house. A car drove past and Rogan stepped up onto the curb, as an arc of slush rose then fell around us. When the car's taillights receded into the night, Rogan turned and started toward Fairview. I ran to keep up with him.

He said, "Don't do it."

"What?"

"Just tell them you won't go." He didn't look at me. "That's all. Just tell them no."

I stared at my feet.

"They can't make you," he said. "Not unless you let them. They can't force you to go."

"I know."

"I wouldn't go. If it was me." A chunk of ice went skidding in front of us as he kicked furiously at the ground. "If they tried to make me go without you. I wouldn't do it."

He turned to me. His eyes looked flat and gray, all the color leached from them. "Maddy."

"I know," I whispered. "I know."

We'd reached the porch. Rogan stood with his hand on the ornate knob of the front door and looked back at me.

"Aunt Kate." He bared his teeth in a grimace. "Aunt Fate. I can't believe you're going to fucking roll over and do what she says."

He went inside, letting the door fall closed on me.

"Rogan. Stop—"

He ignored me and ran upstairs. I followed, not daring to speak again till we reached the third floor. "Rogan, please."

I tried to grab his hand but he pushed me away and headed for his room. "Rogan—"

He stopped in the doorway. "Oh, fuck."

I came up behind him and stopped.

The room had been trashed. Rogan's mattress lay beneath the window, sheets ripped from it and the ticking slashed open. A chair had been smashed against the wall until its legs shattered, a sheet wrapped around it like a torn sail. Books were everywhere, their pages gone, and empty cardboard boxes, ruined Christmas decorations and Halloween masks and ragged pieces of velvet and lace. Fistfuls of coins were strewn across the floor.

Only when I stumbled inside, I saw they weren't coins but foil-wrapped condoms. The air reeked of scorched wool. Ashes covered the floor, and blackened fragments of charred wood; cigarette butts and rolling papers and broken glass ornaments.

"Oh, no," whispered Rogan. "Oh, no, oh, no."

He knelt beside the entrance to the attic. The door had been torn from its hinges. It dangled from the wall, surrounded by crushed cartons and a splintered wooden panel. On the floor was a heap of shredded paper.

"Maddy." Rogan gathered the wreckage in his hands and looked up at me. "Oh, Maddy."

It was all that remained of the theater: ragged bits of cardboard and tissue, traces of glitter falling from the shattered awning of what had once been the proscenium. I dropped beside Rogan and raked through the drift of torn paper, trying to find something that had not been destroyed.

But there was only shredded cardboard and gilt, matchstick-size splinters that had been topiary trees and damp gauze bearing the faintest shadow of a ship's mast.

"Who—"

Before I could shape the question, someone grabbed Rogan and dragged him to his feet.

"*Do you think this is a flophouse?*" I stumbled backward as my uncle shouted, his face so red it looked as though it had been boiled. "*Do you think this is your crash pad? Do you?*"

His hand struck Rogan's cheek. My cousin reeled backward and struck the wall. *"You left a cigarette burning in there! You nearly burned the house down—the whole goddamn house—"*

"Stop," I yelled. "Stop, you can't—"

My uncle turned and stared at me, his eyes widening in revulsion.

"You get out of here." He began pushing me toward the door. "Get out of here, get out of here—"

I tripped and nearly fell, caught myself, and staggered onto the landing. Rogan got to his feet and looked around wildly until he saw me.

"Maddy," he said. "Go—"

I fled downstairs and back outside. I didn't stop until I reached my own house, empty and dark in the early January night.

It wasn't until much later, when I looked out toward Fairview and the carriage house beyond, that I saw both houses were dark as well. For the first time I could remember, no ghost light burned in Aunt Kate's upper window.

❖ ❖ ❖

I DIDN'T SEE ROGAN AGAIN BEFORE I LEFT FOR London. His parents pulled him from St. Brendan's and sent him to board at Mount St. Michael Academy, an all-boy school in the Bronx run by Marist Brothers. We were forbidden to write or call each other.

The truth was that, after three or four days, I was too caught up in a rush of preparation to grieve.

And I was young—I was constantly reminded how young I was, as though somehow my age made an invalid of me.

It didn't, of course. I knew I was being pushed away from Rogan, not just his physical being but his memory, everything connected with him. Which was absurd—he was my cousin; we were tied by blood if nothing else: our shared childhoods, our shared neighborhood, our parents and siblings, the very air we'd breathed for fifteen years—all of these things bound us intrinsically. It was a temporary separation: a few months, a year. Until we were older. Nothing would ever change.

But everything did.

That spring, Uncle Richard and Aunt Pat separated. Within a year, they were divorced—the first divorce in the Tierney clan. My parents didn't separate, but during my second term at the National Youth Theatre they moved. The house at Arden Terrace was sold, a new house bought in a small town fifty miles north of where I'd grown up.

I was seventeen before I spent a night in it. My visits to the United States were few and short-lived. I don't know what strings Aunt Kate pulled to get me into the London theater scene, but once she tugged at them, she never let go. Her friend in Hampstead extended his Greek visit by eighteen months, so we remained in his flat, part of a lovely gray stone edifice surrounded by holly trees and rhododendron that bloomed all year long. At drama school I was a quick study; neither brilliant nor beautiful but willing to take on any role, no matter how dour, no matter what short notice.

"A character actor" I was told when, after three years, I finally auditioned for Central. I'd done Viola, and Amanda from *Private Lives*, for my audition at RADA—I now had a perfect English accent—but I wasn't accepted there. Central took me, though. Despite being typed as a character actress, I did my share of ingenues, along with the classics, in school productions of many of the same plays I'd seen years earlier with Aunt Kate and Rogan. Shakespeare, Shaw, Wycherley, Noël Coward's *Hay Fever*, and Alan Ayckbourn's *Norman Conquests*. My parents flew over to see *Hay Fever*, and once VCRs and videotape became popular, I sent them tapes of everything I did.

Aunt Kate was back in the States by then. I moved from Hampstead to share a flat with several other struggling actors in Highgate, all of whom were gratifyingly envious when I got a small role at the Royal Court with Nancy Meckler. A year later, I toured with the Manchester Royal Exchange in *Charlie's Aunt* with Sabrina Franklin, saving enough money to buy a one-bedroom flat near the Angel in Islington. To distinguish myself from my great-grandmother, I performed under the name Madeline Armin.

By the early 1980s I was doing a lot of television work. A girl who got run over by a tram in *Rumpole of the Bailey*, a running part on the soap opera *Emmerdale*, and a nice bit as a female police rookie on *Juliet Bravo*. It wasn't what I'd dreamed of doing, but it was what I'd trained for. I wasn't a star yet. I was something that occasionally seemed even more miraculous, especially among my cohort: a working actor. Still in my twenties, I was young enough to believe that greater success would come; that I wouldn't be frozen forever in those small moments on BBC1; that another, hidden world still awaited me, populated with the parts I was meant to play

Desdemona, Lady Macbeth, Noël Coward's Gilda, and yes, Viola.

In the mid-1980s I went to Washington, D.C., for several months, after being cast in a supporting role in *The Good Person of Szechuan* at Arena Stage. I saw Rogan then, for the first time since leaving Yonkers. I'd kept up with his whereabouts through my parents and my sister Brigid. I'd learned not to ask Aunt Kate for news, after she made a brief trip to visit me several years earlier.

"Your cousin Rogan's not doing well, Maddy." She shook her head and stared down at the rhododendrons glistening silvery green in a late November rain. "You know he's a heroin addict, right?"

I turned so she wouldn't see my face.

"No," I said. "I knew he was in a band. I thought they were doing pretty well; Brigid said they had a record deal."

"I saw him at Pat's house and he looked awful. Jaundiced." Aunt Kate's mouth tightened. "Someone should help him. One of his brothers."

I slid a headshot into an envelope and said nothing.

Now, at last, I would see him. I took the train to New York and met him for lunch, all the time I could steal from work. I had suggested Rosoff's.

"Nah. There's a good Szechuan place near Penn Station. In honor of your play." He laughed and gave me the address. Through the telephone I heard the familiar *phhtt* of a match being struck, an indrawn breath. "Go there. I'll meet you at one thirty."

He sat at a table near the front of the restaurant, a narrow steam-filled place where there was more food on the shag carpeting than the tables. "Hey, Maddy."

I could feel him flinch as I put my arms around him.

"Rogan." I pulled back to look at him. "Hi, Rogan, hi . . ."

Someone had set fire to him and burned away all his youth. The nimbus of golden hair had faded to dull russet, close-cropped and already receding. He was gaunt, his skin so thin I could see the capillaries beneath, a faint blue fretwork starred here and there with red where the vessels had burst. There were already lines across his brow and deep grooves beside his mouth.

And yet he remained beautiful. Not only to me: I saw the waitress stare at him after she'd taken our drink orders and returned to the bar, and the bartender as well, watching us as we ate. His pallor only accentuated his eyes, their aquamarine now darkened to a cold teal blue, and the delicate line of his jaw and cheekbones.

"You look good," I said.

He gave me a twisted smile. "You, too."

I stared at his beat-up leather jacket and T-shirt, scuffed engineer's boots, and filthy jeans. In D.C. the weather had been sultry; I wore a white linen shirtdress and espadrilles, clothes that had seemed elegant, even sexy, when I got on the train at Union Station.

Now I felt dowdy and middle-aged, far older than twenty-six. Beside Rogan I looked ancient.

We made desultory conversation while we ate. I downplayed my modest success, which wasn't hard. I hadn't had a leading role since drama school, and the TV shows I'd appeared in weren't yet broadcast in the United States. Rogan told me about his band's recent gigs in the city and Philadelphia and Boston. I'd imagined this reunion for years, and for the last few weeks had been almost sick with anticipation and yearning—how could a few hours on a Monday afternoon even begin to be enough time to knit our lives back together?

The lunch was excruciating. Rogan wouldn't meet my eyes. I asked after his family and he shrugged.

"I don't see them. You're the first one I've talked to in, I dunno, seven years."

When I mentioned Aunt Kate in passing, he grimaced.

"Aunt Fate." His face contorted into a mask of loathing. "Fucking bitch. I don't want to hear about her."

We finished eating. I picked up the check. Only after we were back outside did he touch me, pulling me to him and resting his head lightly on my shoulder.

"Maddy. Thanks for coming up to see me." His tone grew slightly mocking. "It's been a really long time. We're both so busy."

He drew away and reached into the pocket of his leather jacket. "You have a tape player?"

I nodded. "Yeah, a Walkman."

"Here." He handed me an audiocassette. "This is a demo we're putting together. It's really rough, but it'll give you an idea anyway. Sounds a lot better live. You should come hear us sometime."

"I will. You should come see the play."

His eyes grew distant. "Yeah, maybe." He lit a cigarette and looked in the direction of Penn Station. "You better go or you'll miss your train. I'd walk you over but I have to meet someone."

My mouth was dry as I leaned in to kiss him. He gave me a small half smile, turning his head so my lips brushed his cheek.

"See you," he said softly, and walked away.

On the Metroliner back to D.C., I sat beside the window and listened to his tape. A mix of original songs and covers, "Helter Skelter" and "Turn Blue" and "Panic in the World." I had expected his voice to be raw or smoke-coarsened.

But then I punched the Play button and felt my skin grow cold as that same pure, high tenor rang out, so wild and true and utterly unchanged it was like being thrust back onstage with him. I shut my eyes and played the tape over and over, until the train at last pulled into Union Station. I gathered my things, a sheaf of unread scripts and magazines, shoved them into my bag with my Walkman, and made my way to my sublet apartment on Capitol Hill.

❖ ❖ ❖

I HAD ALWAYS IMAGINED MY CAREER WOULD BE like a series of rehearsals leading up to opening night, followed by a long run and longer semiretirement, with turns as Lady Bracknell and Juliet's Nurse to buttress solid employment in a critically acclaimed television series or maybe even a movie.

Instead it was an endless audition; a few nice parts in regional theaters before I turned thirty and, almost overnight, the leading roles disappeared. I became trapped in the career immurement that awaits a character actor, shuttling between London and New York, theater and bit parts in TV. Usually I was better than the shows I was in; always I imagined someone else on the stage with me, Rogan's flickering image like the static on a dead television channel, his voice in my head long after the tape he'd given me wore out from being played and replayed for so many years.

When my work was reviewed, critics marveled how I inevitably triumphed over bad material, especially if I shared the stage with weak leading men; how it seemed as if my own presence animated the air between us, as if someone else, something else, moved there unseen.

Even in this feeble attempt at a post-Stoppard black comedy
of manners, the redoubtable Madeline Armin walks the stage
like a woman possessed.

But I would never be a star. Maybe there's only a certain amount of talent that can go around, especially in a family like ours; maybe after hundreds of years, the Tierney gifts had finally died out. Whatever acting talent I possessed, it wasn't enough. I channeled all my energy into my work. I had a few halfhearted relationships, and a drawn-out affair with a married woman, an actress I continued to work with, off and on, until her career outstripped mine. I still read about her occasionally, small items in *Time Out* or *Vanity Fair*. In love, as in theater, I had never had any magic.

True, I never flamed out. And I never shone, not even for a moment, the way my cousin had.

❖ ❖ ❖

DECADES PASSED. MY PARENTS RETIRED AND MOVED
from New York to Arizona. When Rogan's mother died, I sent him a
note of condolence from London, carefully scripted and written on
thick Crane stationery. I never received a reply. A few years later, my
father told me that Uncle Richard had cancer. Within several months
he, too, was dead. This time I didn't write.

The houses on Arden Terrace had long since been sold, all save
Fairview and Aunt Kate's carriage house. Two of the bigger heaps were
torn down and McMansions built in their stead, but most of the others were restored and carefully maintained by doctors and lawyers and
stockbrokers, the same sorts of people who had first colonized Arden
Terrace at the beginning of the last century. Aunt Kate remained in
her home, attended by a series of loyal and well-paid home health
aides who read to her when her vision deteriorated and made certain
there was a good supply of audiobooks and cognac when they left at
night to their own homes in the Bronx or White Plains.

I visited her whenever I was in New York, but that wasn't often
now. I had no work in the city; not much in London, either. I did
a series of audiobooks, adaptations of a successful children's series
about a brave ant, and that made me enough money to live on.

When I did visit my aunt, the relative prosperity of her home, and
the rest of Arden Terrace, made Fairview's gradual decay seem even
worse. After Uncle Richard's death, the mansion had been inherited
by his sons.

But no one wanted to live in it. Despite a few prosperous neighborhoods, like Arden Terrace, Yonkers had become a ghost city. Gentrification was still a ways off. My cousins were comfortably ensconced in Westchester or Putnam County with their families.

All save Rogan.

Over the years, news of him had filtered to me through family members. Like me, he never married. For twenty years he lived in the city, singing in various incarnations of his original band. He drifted from apartment to apartment downtown and, when he was finally priced out of the East Village, into Brooklyn. In the early 1990s he almost died. I learned about this only a few years afterward, and it was never clear to me what had happened. AIDS, I thought, and felt that same chill as when I'd first heard him sing.

But it wasn't AIDS.

"He's in the hospital," Aunt Kate told me over the phone. Her voice was so frail I didn't ask her to repeat herself. I was afraid she'd lose the strength to talk at all.

As a result, during the next year I received only fractured accounts of my cousin. Rehab. Another hospitalization, a second stint at rehab. Then, surprisingly, a performance at a Tom Waits tribute, or maybe Tom Waits had sung at a benefit for Rogan?

Aunt Kate herself seemed uncertain. She sounded more drifty these days, which was to be expected. I asked her, more than once, how old she was.

She never answered. She had always seemed ageless to me, younger than my own parents. Still, no matter how I did the math, I figured she had to be well into her nineties, if not over a hundred.

After 9/11 she grew even more remote: one of my in-laws had been trapped in the towers, and the husband of Aunt Kate's favorite caregiver. I spoke to her less frequently, on her birthday and at Christmas. Finally, six years later, I received a phone call from my father saying she had died.

It was the end of December, the middle of a harsh winter in the Northeast. My parents were too frail to make the trip from Sedona, my sisters too caught up with the aftermath of Christmas and their own children and grandchildren. The rest of the Tierneys were scattered and long out of touch.

So I told my father I'd fly over from London to represent the family at the funeral Mass at St. Brendan's. It was only after I hung up that I realized I'd forgotten to ask what time the funeral was; also, where I could stay?

I rang my father back.

"Your cousin Rogan's made all the arrangements," he said. "He stayed with her, you know. He was there in the hospital when she died. Your mother e-mailed and told him you're coming. Have a safe trip, dear."

My plane was late. It was a cloudless blue day. Flying above the Canadian Maritimes and New England, I saw snow thirty thousand feet below, a wrinkled white expanse of woodland dulling into gray urban sprawl, pocked with frozen lakes and reservoirs. In the minutes I stood outside at Kennedy before locating my hired car, my lungs ached from the cold.

"Fucking freezing," the driver told me as we headed toward the city. "Too cold to snow, even. Where's our global warming?"

The car took me directly to St. Brendan's. There had been no wake, and only a few people were inside the church when I arrived. The two middle-aged women I assumed were Aunt Kate's health aides, and the ancient couple I remembered from my own tenure at St. Brendan's.

And Rogan.

"Maddy." He stood in the first pew and waved me toward him. "Jesus, Maddy, I can't believe you came all this way, in this weather."

He was thin, though not gaunt as he'd been twenty years before. He wore a black woolen overcoat over faded corduroys, and a gray henley shirt. His thin russet hair had burned to ash; his eyes were a pale washed turquoise, slightly bloodshot; his face was heavily lined. He looked ravaged; still beautiful, still wrecked.

But his arms around me were strong, and when he drew me to sit in the pew beside him his hand held mine, tightly, until the priest made the final benediction.

Afterward I rode with Rogan to Valhalla for the burial, a ceremony that lasted a fraction as long as the drive there, then back to Yonkers, braving the frigid cold with my window open while Rogan chain-smoked.

"She talked about you all the time," he said on the way home. We hadn't spoken much till then, but it wasn't an uncomfortable silence; more a sort of intermission, while we looked at each other and grew accustomed to once again breathing the same air. "She was really proud of you. The first Tierney in a hundred years to be onstage again."

"Not a hundred years." I gazed out the window. We were on North Broadway, passing houses and storefronts strung with Christmas lights. A bar was hosting a karaoke Kwanzaa contest. "Madeline wasn't that long ago. And you were onstage. With your bands, I mean. That's performing."

"Not to her it wasn't." He laughed, a faint edge of bitterness to his voice, and tossed his cigarette out the window. "Your TV stuff, that wasn't, either. *Rumpole of the Bailey* or whatever the hell it was. None of that stuff counted. Only the stage. Only the *theater.*"

He pronounced it as our great-grandmother might have, *thee-ah-tuh*. "That was the only thing that mattered to Aunt Fate."

We pulled into Arden Terrace. I sat beside him, my heart beating too fast, fear and anticipation and jet lag all crowded into that small car. "How long did you live with her?"

"Two years. Two and a half. I didn't actually live with her, not in her house. She had Luisa and Jadeis for that. They're the health-care professionals." He gave another sharp laugh. "I live at Fairview. I'm, like, the caretaker—Michael and the rest of them, they pay me to stay there and keep it from falling into the ground. Which is a losing fucking proposition, I can tell you. But it's great for me; I can work on my music or whatever, no one hassles me. I never even have to fucking see them. Here we are—"

He slowed in front of the house where I'd grown up. "They shingled it about ten years ago," he said, peering out the side window. "It looked good. Now it looks like it needs some paint. But that's nothing compared to my house. Which looks like the Munsters live there."

The car turned down the long drive to Fairview.

"No kidding," I said.

It didn't look completely derelict, just neglected and sad. Shingles were missing, leaving long gaps like rows of rotted teeth. Plywood covered one of the upper windows, and mats of dead wisteria hung like wet carpet from the porch railings. A few lights glimmered downstairs.

"Aunt Kate's place is in better shape," said Rogan as he parked. "She put a lot of money into it."

I stepped out, shivering, and got my bag from the backseat. "What's going to happen to it now?"

Rogan locked the car and waited for me before heading for the front door. "Actually," he said, sounding embarrassed, "she left it to me."

"Really?" I felt a momentary spike of jealousy, then laughed. "But that's great! Her stuff, too? All those things of Madeline's and, well, everything?"

"Yeah. We went through most of it before she died. She wanted to give it to a museum, or a college—I must've called every school in New York. No one was interested. SUNY Purchase took a few things. I gave some of it to the girls who took care of her—nothing you'd want, just some furniture, blankets, and stuff like that. The rest I packed up. I figured you'd want to look at it and maybe take some of it back to England with you."

"Maybe," I said. "I don't have a lot of room. And, you know, I'm not a citizen. Which these days makes it hard. And it's getting expensive. I don't know how long I can really afford to stay there."

We stepped inside. Rogan switched on a light as I rubbed my arms. "Jesus, it's as cold here as outside."

"Yeah, sorry. Here, I'll put the heat on."

He went into the hall, returning a minute later. "I can't really afford to live here, either." He laughed. "But hey, as long as Michael keeps writing the checks, I'll keep it warm. You hungry?"

I followed him into the kitchen. It was like walking through a haunted house of my own life. Most of the furniture was gone, as well as the worn Turkish carpets and mirrors and ancient theatrical memorabilia.

But enough remained that it was still, recognizably, Rogan's home. Most of the damage seemed to be limited to the house's exterior; the structure was still sound. Rogan showed me where he'd made repairs to the interior walls, replaced some of the old windows with triple-insulated glass, and done a serviceable job of patching a crack in the plaster in the kitchen. There was even a bedraggled Christmas tree in the living room, strung with a few strands of those big, old, multicolored bulbs that are no longer fashionable, and hung with glass ornaments.

"I saved those," he said as we stood and admired the tree. He turned back to the kitchen and began to make coffee and sandwiches from leftover turkey. "After my father went crazy that time and trashed everything. I think that's when my mother finally decided she'd had enough. Not when he was pounding the shit out of me. When he broke all the Christmas decorations."

"Jesus, Rogan."

I sat at the table, still in my coat. He handed me a mug of coffee, turned down the dimmer on the overhead light, and lit a candle in a blue glass holder.

"Hey. I remember that," I said softly. "That was under the porch . . ."

He seemed not to hear me. "Forget it. It's history. You want a sweater? It'll warm up soon. Last winter I put in a new furnace. Aunt Fate paid for it; Michael was too cheap. I told him when the pipes burst and he had to put in a new foundation he'd wish he'd popped for a furnace, but he said if that happened he'd just tear the whole fucking place down. He would, too. No one cares about this place but me."

He turned and looked at me. He'd removed his coat and, despite the chill, pushed up the sleeves of his shirt, so that I could see how the hairs on his arms glowed in the candlelight. I reached out and touched his wrist, like mine only bigger, took his hand, and laid mine beside it.

"We could have been twins," I said. "I wonder if it would have been different. If there had been a girl in your family."

"They were wrong about that, too." He stared at our hands, then linked his fingers with mine. "All that stuff about us. All that boatload of guilt. People marry their cousins; it's not even illegal. I know a guy in Bay Ridge, he's married to his cousin. Not that he tells anyone," he added and smiled ruefully. "You want a drink?"

He opened a bottle of wine. We ate our turkey sandwiches, and then Rogan handed me a CD.

"Check this out."

The cover was a black-and-white photo of an empty city street, a figure silhouetted beneath a lamppost.

Rogan Tierney: Sad Songs.

I looked at him. "This is you?"

He grinned. "Hey, write what you know."

I turned it over and read the back. "Jesus—Nicky Cox produced this? How'd you get him?" I scanned the rest of the names in disbelief. "How'd you get all these guys?"

"You meet a lot of people at NA meetings in New York. I'll play it for you later. I have a whole little studio upstairs. It's pretty cool."

We finished the wine.

"Is it okay that you do this?" I asked as he set the empty bottle in the sink. "If you're doing that whole Narcotics Anonymous thing?"

"I'm straight, not necessarily sober. But I don't do it much." He shrugged, poured us each a tumbler of Irish Mist, then gazed at the bottle. "This was my father's."

He took his drink and walked to a window overlooking the carriage house, the long sweep of darkness to the Hudson. "He used to drink this stuff after dinner every night. After the cocktails, I mean. I found a stockpile of it after I moved in. I'm working my way through it. Not at his rate, though."

I walked over to stand beside him. Outside the night was so clear and black it looked brittle, as though, like ice, it would shatter if you touched it. Stars seemed to stir in the wind. The ridge of trees that bordered the lawn had become so dense and overgrown you could no longer see the lights of the houses below.

Only in the uppermost window of Aunt Kate's carriage house did a single light glow, pale yellow, and cast a bright lozenge onto the ground.

"You kept it on." I began to cry. "After everything, you were the one—"

"Maddy." He turned and put his arms around me and drew me close. "Don't cry, baby, please don't cry . . ."

He kissed me. He smelled as he always had, of smoke and sweat, his mouth bitter with nicotine. I could feel the wind through the cracks in the walls, and then a slow shifting, as though the entire house moved around us. Behind my closed eyes it all began to take shape again, the carpets in their muted colors unfurling across the wooden floors, white lace curtains at the windows, wisteria blooming on the porch outside, and the echo of footsteps on the stairs above.

"Maddy."

I blinked. There were no curtains at the window, and only worn linoleum underfoot. The kitchen smelled of fuel oil and cigarette smoke.

But Rogan's head rested against mine, and Rogan's voice whispered as he grabbed my hand and stepped away from me.

"Come here," he said. "Upstairs. I want to show you something."

He picked up the candle in its blue glass and walked out of the kitchen, through the hall and into the foyer, and up the curving stairway. I held his hand and hurried after him. On the second-floor landing I peered into a room where a computer blinked on a long trestle table, surrounded by speakers and coils of wire.

"That's the studio," said Rogan. He started up the steps to the third floor. "But that's still not it."

I said nothing, just shivered and followed him. The unsteady candlelight made the dark space seem even colder than the rest of the house. When we reached the third floor, Rogan stopped.

"Close your eyes."

I rubbed my arms. "Do I have to? I can't see anything."

"Yeah. You do. Wait right there."

I flinched as he let go of my hand and stepped away, then shut my eyes. I didn't feel like I had downstairs, when the entire house seemed to knit itself around me. Just cold and a growing unease that was close to dread. I thought of when I had last stood here; of Rogan crouched against the wall and his father shouting at me.

Get out of here, you get out of here . . .

"Come here." I started as Rogan took me by the shoulders. "Keep your eyes closed. It's okay, I won't let you fall. Come here, but don't look until I tell you."

I took tiny baby steps as he led me across the landing, past the door to Michael's bedroom, and into his own.

"Can I open them?" I knew I sounded anxious and drunk, but I didn't care. "Rogan?"

"Hang on, just a sec—"

He stepped away. For a moment I stood alone, fighting the urge to open my eyes, to bolt. Then Rogan was beside me. His arm settled around my shoulders.

"Okay," he said. "You can look."

I opened my eyes and blinked, staring first at the ceiling, then the floor as I tried to get my bearings.

The room was empty. No books, no bed, no rugs, no drapes; no furniture save a makeshift table made of a sheet of plywood on top of a small desk. At its edge glowed a half circle of candles in colored glasses, cobalt and red and green.

"I know it's late," said Rogan. "But Merry Christmas."

I blinked, unsure what I was looking at.

And then I saw.

It was the toy theater, the fairy stage and proscenium we had shared thirty-odd years before. Only it was no longer a thing of light and shadow but a real theater, torn cardboard and paper carefully reassembled, the broken struts and floor repaired, clumsily in spots, with tape and glue and what looked like dirty plaster. The proscenium arch had been so badly damaged that only a small part of it remained, a fragile gilt arc within a crumpled span of tinfoil etched painstakingly with ballpoint ink in the same design that had been on the original. Crepe paper and a ragged fringe of orange silk replaced the curtains. The topiary trees and snow-capped mountains were a pastiche of torn paper and pictures cut from magazines. The scrim was a piece of mosquito netting, painted with a glowing silver moon and the spidery prongs of a broken mast.

"Rogan." It hurt to speak. I stepped toward the table and knelt. "It's—there are people."

And there were. Dozens of figures, each no bigger than my finger, their heads clipped from old photographs and mounted onto stiff paper and cardboard. There were my parents, heads affixed to the gowns of a king and queen; there was Uncle Richard, incongruously smiling above a hunchback's torso, and Aunt Pat in her wedding gown but with a donkey's long muzzle. There was smiling Mr. Sullivan from the St. Brendan's yearbook, his hands raised like a football referee's. There were my sisters, garbed like princesses or stepsisters or shopgirls; and Rogan's brothers, with monkey's tails or Grecian robes. There were all our friends from *Twelfth Night*: dizzy Sir Toby and dopey Duncan Moss; Maria and Fabian and Malvolio; Orsino and Olivia and Sir Andrew Aguecheek.

And there was Aunt Kate, suspended above the stage by a piece of fishing line, with two sets of wings, a swan's and a bat's.

And there was me.

I stood beneath Aunt Kate in my yearbook snapshot, costumed as Viola. But my head had been replaced, so carefully that only I would know that the little figure brandishing her wooden sword didn't bear my fifteen-year-old face, but the delicately made-up features I bore in my *Playbill* photo for *The Good Person of Szechuan*; the adult Viola I had never played.

"Rogan," I whispered.

I stretched out my hand to touch his image. It stood center stage, slightly in front of mine; a Polaroid retouched with ink. He wore the Pierrot's costume from *Twelfth Night*, his head thrown back and eyes closed with the same rapturous expression he had then.

But this photo was new—it might have been taken that day—and when I touched it, I could feel that it was still slightly damp, as though the glue had not yet dried.

Rogan lowered his head to kiss me.

"*And thus the whirligig of time brings in his revenges,*'" he said and began to sing.

"When that I was and a little tiny boy,
With hey, ho, the wind and the rain,
A foolish thing was but a toy,
For the rain it raineth every day."

He sang as he had all those years before; as I'd heard him sing,

night after night, alone in bed in my Islington flat; as I'd heard him
every time I stood offstage, fighting waves of fear until I could take
that first step onto a stage in Manchester or Bristol or D.C. His voice
rang so loudly that the candles guttered in their holders; the dark
room closed around us until I felt the attic walls and in the corners of
my eyes saw sparks of lightning, blue and black and silver.

> *"But when I came unto my beds,*
> *With hey, ho, the wind and the rain,*
> *With tosspots still had drunken heads,*
> *For the rain it raineth every day."*

I blinked. Tears blurred my vision so that it seemed I glimpsed
the resurrected theater through a snow-covered window. I rubbed my
eyes, then gasped.

It was snowing: tiny whirling flakes like glitter or talc but cold,
and wet—snow, real snow, impossible snow, falling in a moonlit col-
umn from the ceiling onto the paper stage as Rogan sang.

> *"A great while ago the world begun,*
> *With hey, ho, the wind and the rain,*
> *But that's all one, our play is done,*
> *And we'll strive to please you every day."*

The eddies rose and fell with my cousin's voice, sweeping over
all of us in waves, matchstick trees and painted moon and cardboard

figures in a toy theater, snow and shipwreck and stage all whorled together into one great bright storm with Rogan and me at its center, motionless in our embrace, long after his voice fell silent, long after first light struck the stony face of the Palisades and the frozen river far below.

ABOUT THE AUTHOR

BORN IN SAN DIEGO, ELIZABETH HAND GREW UP IN

Yonkers and Pound Ridge, New York, before heading to Washington, D.C., to study playwriting and anthropology at Catholic University. For a number of years she worked at the Smithsonian's National Air & Space Museum, but in 1988 quit her job to write full-time and moved to the coast of Maine, where she lived in a four-hundred-square-foot lakefront cottage with no indoor plumbing or running water (it now has both, and is her office).

The author of ten novels and three collections of short fiction, she received the inaugural Shirley Jackson Award for best work of psychological suspense for her most recent book, *Generation Loss*. Her fiction has also received two Nebula Awards, three World Fantasy Awards, two International Horror Guild Awards, the James M. Tiptree, Jr. Award, and the Mythopoeic Fantasy Award, and in 2001 she was the recipient of an Individual Artist Fellowship in Literature from the Maine Arts Commission/NEA. She is a longtime reviewer and critic whose work appears regularly in the *Washington Post*, the *Village Voice*, Salon.com, *Fantasy & Science Fiction*, and the *Boston Globe*, among others. She has two teenage children and continues to live in Maine, where she is at work on her next novel.

Her Web site is www.elizabethhand.com, and she blogs at community.livejournal.com/theinferior4.